"You're just another client to me."

"I haven't said I want to be anything else," Brant remarked.

"Good," she said viciously. "You're in room 9—here's your key."

She was holding it in her fingertips. To test his immunity to her, Brant deliberately closed his hand over hers, and as soon as he'd done so, knew he'd made a very bad mistake. Her skin was warm and smooth, with that supple strength he'd forgotten.

He snatched the key from her. Rowan hurried past him and unlocked the door to room 10, entered the room and shut the door with rather more force than was necessary.

Brant stood very still under the moon. He wanted Rowan—in his bed, in his arms, where she belonged—and to hell with the divorce. How was he going to get a minute's sleep, knowing she was on the other side of the wall from him?

Although born in England, SANDRA FIELD has
lived most of her life in Canada; she says the
silence and emptiness of the north speaks to
her particularly. While she enjoys traveling, and
passing on her sense of a new place, she often
chooses to write about the city that is now her
home. Sandra says, "I write out of my experience. I have learned that love with its joys and its
pains is all-important. I hope this knowledge
enriches my writing, and touches a chord in you,
the reader."

Books by Sandra Field

SANDRA FIELD

Remarried in Haste

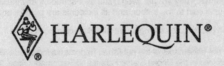

TORONTO • NEW YORK • LONDON
AMSTERDAM • PARIS • SYDNEY • HAMBURG
STOCKHOLM • ATHENS • TOKYO • MILAN • MADRID
PRAGUE • WARSAW • BUDAPEST • AUCKLAND

ISBN 0-373-12042-7

REMARRIED IN HASTE

First North American Publication 1999.

PROLOGUE

"IT'S time you go and see your wife, Brant."

The rounded beach stone Brant had been idly playing with slipped from his fingers and fell to the floor. The noise it made seemed disproportionately loud, jarring his nerves. He bent to pick it up and said coolly, "I don't have a wife."

Equally coolly, Gabrielle said, "Her name's Rowan."

"We're divorced. As well you know."

Gabrielle Doucette was leaning back in her seat, her legs slung carelessly over one arm of the chair; her bundled black hair and deep blue eyes were very familiar to him, as was her ability to look totally relaxed in tense situations. "Sometimes," she said, "a divorce is just a legal document, a piece of paper with printing on it. Nothing to do with the heart."

"I was legally separated for a year, and I've been divorced for fourteen months," Brant said tightly. "In all that time I've neither heard from Rowan nor seen her. Her lawyer sent back my first batch of support checks with a letter that told me, more or less politely, to get lost. The letter with the second batch was considerably less polite. All of which, to my mind, indicates something a little more significant than a mere legal document."

Gabrielle stared thoughtfully into her glass of wine; they had eaten bouillabaisse, which was her specialty, and had moved from the table to sit by the window of her Toronto condominium, which overlooked the constant traffic of the 401. "On her part, maybe."

"On mine, too." Brant tipped back his glass, draining it. "When are you going to produce the delectable dessert I know you've got hidden away somewhere in the refrigerator?"

"When I'm ready." She smiled at him, a smile of genuine affection. "You and I were thrown together for eight months under circumstances that were far from ordinary—"

"That's the understatement of the year," he said; the stinking cells, the oppressive heat, the inevitable illnesses to which they'd both succumbed had been quite extraordinarily unpleasant. Not to say life-threatening.

"—Yet you never fell in love with me."

He opted for a partial truth; he had no intention of telling her certain of the reasons why he hadn't fallen in love with her, they were entirely too personal. "I knew you weren't available," he said. "You still haven't gotten over Daniel's death." Daniel had been her husband of seven years, who'd died in a car accident before Brant had met Gabrielle.

"True enough."

He looked around the stark and ultramodern room. "Besides, I don't like your taste in furniture."

She chuckled. "That, also, is true. But I think there's another reason. You didn't fall in love with me because you still love Rowan."

Brant had seen this coming. Keeping his hands loose on the stem of his glass, he said, "You're missing out by being a labor negotiator, Gabrielle—you should be writing fiction."

"And how would you feel if you heard Rowan was about to remarry?"

His whole body went rigid; for a split second he was twenty-six years old again, back in Angola that sultry evening when a live grenade had arched gracefully through the air toward him and his feet had felt like lumps of concrete. He rasped, "*Is* she? Who told you?"

Gabrielle smiled again, a rather smug smile. "So you do care. I thought you did."

"Very clever," Brant said, making no attempt to mask his anger; he and Gabrielle had long ago passed the point of being polite to each other for the sake of outward appearances.

"It's bound to happen sooner or later," Gabrielle continued placidly. "Rowan is a beautiful and talented young woman."

"What she does with her life is nothing to do with me."

Quite suddenly Gabrielle snapped her glass down on the chrome-edged table beside her. "All right—I'll stop playing games. I've watched you the last two years. You've been acting like a man possessed. Like a man who couldn't care less if he got himself killed. Any ordinary person would have been dead five times over with some of the things you've done, the situations you've exposed yourself to since you and Rowan split up." Her voice broke very slightly. "I don't want to pick up the paper one day and find myself reading your obituary."

Brant said blankly, for it was a possibility that had never occurred to him before, "You're not in love with *me*, are you?"

He looked so horrified that genuine amusement lightened her features. "Of course not. Someday I'm sure I'll fall in love again, it would be an insult to Daniel's memory if I didn't. But it won't be with you, Brant."

"You had me worried for a moment."

"And if you're trying to change the subject," Gabrielle went on with considerable determination, "it won't work. I *know* you still love Rowan. After all, you and I virtually lived together for the eight months we were held for ransom, I had lots of opportunity to observe you. One of the things that kept you sane through that terrible time was the knowledge you'd be going home to Rowan. Your wife.''

Through gritted teeth Brant said, ''Your imagination's operating overtime.''

Imperturbably Gabrielle went on, ''And then we were released unexpectedly. When you got home she was leading a tour in Greenland, and when she got back from there her lawyer made it all too clear that Rowan wanted nothing to do with you because she thought you and I were a number. You wouldn't let me go and see her to try and explain— oh, no, you were much too proud for that. In fact, you made me swear I wouldn't get in touch with her at all, stiff-necked idiot that you are. So you lost her. And you've never stopped grieving that loss. I know you haven't. I'd swear it in court on a stack of Bibles as high as this building.''

''Dammit, I'm divorced! And that's the way I like it.''

''Don't lie to me.''

He surged to his feet. ''I've had enough of this—I'm getting out of here.''

''Can't take the heat? Afraid you might have to admit to emotions? You, Brant Curtis, feeling pain because a woman left you?'' She swung her legs to the floor and stood up, too, with a touch of awkwardness that reminded him, sharply and painfully, of Rowan's sudden, coltlike movements. ''I know you have feelings,'' Gabrielle announced, ''even if I don't know why you've repressed them so drastically they don't have the slightest chance of escaping...sort of like us in that awful cell. You have them, though—and they're killing you.''

''You've got a great touch with purple prose.''

''So you're a coward,'' she said flatly.

Her words bit deep into a place Brant rarely acknowledged to himself and certainly never would to anyone else. Of course he wasn't a coward. If anything, he was the exact opposite, a man who continually took risks for the highs they gave him. He headed for the door, throwing the words over his shoulder. "Remind me the next time you invite me for dinner to say no."

"You need to see Rowan!"

"I don't know where she is and I'm not going looking for her!"

"I know where she is." Gabrielle turned and from a wrought-iron shelf picked up a folded brochure, waving it in the air. "In three days she'll be leading a small group of people through various islands in the West Indies looking for endemic birds. Which, in case you didn't know, means birds native to the area. I had to look it up."

In spite of himself, Brant's eyes had flown to the folded piece of paper and his feet had glued themselves to the parquet floor. Conquering the urge to snatch the brochure from her, he rapped, "So what?"

"There's a vacancy on that trip. My friend Sonia's husband—Rick Williams—was to have gone, but he's come down with a bad respiratory infection. You could take his place."

His mouth dry, Brant sneered, "Me? Looking for endemic birds on those cute little Caribbean islands? That's like telling a mercenary soldier he's going back to kindergarten."

"You'd be looking for your wife, Brant." Gabrielle's smile was ironic. "Looking for your life, Brant. You didn't know I was a poet, did you?"

"You've been watching too many soap operas."

"Kindly don't insult me!"

His lashes flickered. Gabrielle almost never lost her temper; unlike Rowan, who lost it frequently.

Rowan. He'd always loved her name. His first gift to her had been a pair of earrings he'd had designed especially for her, little enameled bunches of the deep orange berries of the rowan tree, berries as fiery-colored as her tumbled, shoulder-length hair. Spread on the pillow, her hair had had the glow of fire....

With an exclamation of disgust, because many months ago he'd rigorously trained himself to forget everything that had happened between him and Rowan in their big bed, he held out his hand. Gabrielle passed him the brochure. Brant flattened it; from long years of hiding anything remotely like fear, his hands were as steady as if he were unfolding the daily newspaper. "'Endemic Birds of the Eastern Caribbean,'" he read. "'Guided by Rowan Carter.'"

She'd kept her own name even when they'd been married. For business reasons, she'd said. Although afterward, when she'd left him, he'd wondered if it had been for other, more hidden and more complicated reasons.

He cleared his throat. "You're suggesting I phone the company Rowan works for and propose myself as a substitute for your friend's husband? Rowan, as I recall, has a fair bit of say about the trips she runs—the last person in the world she'd allow to go on one of them would be me."

"Don't tell her. Just turn up."

His jaw dropped. For the space of a full five seconds he looked at Gabrielle in silence. "Intrigue," he said, "that's what you should be writing."

"Rick can cancel easily enough—he bought insurance and he'll get his money back. Or you can pay him for the trip and go in his place. All you'd have to do is change the airline tickets to your name."

"So I'd turn up at the airport in—" he ran his eyes down the page "—Grenada, and say, 'Oh, by the way, Rowan, Rick couldn't make it so I thought I'd come instead.'" He gave an unamused bark of laughter. "She'd throw me on the first plane back to Toronto."

"Then it'll be up to you to convince her otherwise."

"You've never met her—you have no idea how stubborn she can be."

"Like calls to like?" Gabrielle asked gently.

"Oh, do shut up," he snapped. "Of course I'm not going, it's a crazy idea." Nevertheless, with a detached part of his brain, Brant noticed he hadn't put the brochure back on the shelf. Or—more appropriately—thrown it to the floor and trampled on it.

"I made tiramisu for dessert. And I'll put the coffee on."

Gabrielle vanished into the kitchen. Like a man who couldn't help himself, Brant started reading the description of the trip that would be leaving on Wednesday. Seven different islands, two nights on each except for the final island of Antigua, where a one-night stopover was scheduled. Hiking in rain forests and mangrove swamps, opportunities for swimming and snorkeling.

Opportunities for being with Rowan.

For two whole weeks.

He was mad to even consider it. Rowan didn't want anything to do with him, she'd made that abundantly clear. So why set himself up for another rejection when he was doing just fine as he was?

Because he *was* doing fine. Gabrielle's imagination was way out of line with all her talk of love and needs and repressions. He didn't need Rowan any more than Rowan needed him.

He'd hated it when his checks had been returned by that smooth-tongued bastard of a lawyer. Hated not knowing where she was living. Hated it most of all that she'd never wanted to see him again.

But he'd gotten over that. Gotten over it and gone on with his life, the only kind of life he thrived on.

The last thing he needed was to see Rowan again.

What he needed was a cup of strong black coffee and a bowl of tiramisu laden with marscapone. Brant tossed the brochure onto the dining room table and followed Gabrielle into the kitchen.

CHAPTER ONE

AT THIRTY-seven thousand feet the clouds looked solid enough to walk on, and the sky was a guileless blue. Brant stretched his legs into the comfortable amount of space his executive seat allowed him and gazed out of the window. He was flying due south, nonstop, from Toronto to Antigua; in Antigua he'd board a short hop to Grenada.

Where Rowan should be on hand to meet him.

Among the various documents Rick had given him had been a list of participants; he, Brant, was the only Canadian other than Rowan on the trip. Therefore, he'd presumably be the only one coming in on that particular flight; the rest of the group would fly via Puerto Rico or Miami.

It should be an interesting meeting.

Which didn't answer the question of why he was going to Grenada.

His dinner with Gabrielle had been last Sunday. On Monday he'd phoned Rick's wife Sonia and told her he'd take Rick's tickets. On Tuesday his boss—that enigmatic figure who owned and managed an international, prestigious and highly influential magazine of political commentary—had sent a fax requesting him to go to Myanmar, as Burma was now known, and write an article on the heroin trade. Whereupon Brant had almost phoned Sonia back. He liked going to Myanmar, it had that constant miasma of danger on which he flourished. His whole life revolved around places like that.

Grenada wouldn't make the list of the world's most dangerous places. Not by a long shot.

13

So why was he going to Grenada and not Myanmar?

To prove himself right, he thought promptly. To prove he no longer had any feelings for Rowan.

Yeah? He was spending one hell of a lot of money to prove something he'd told Gabrielle didn't need proving.

And why did he, right now, have that sensation of super-vigilance, of every nerve keyed to its highest pitch, the very same feeling that always accompanied him on his assignments?

Don't try and answer that one, Brant Curtis, he told himself ironically, watching a cloud drift by that had the hooked neck and forked tongue of a prehistoric sea monster. He'd told his boss he had plans for a well-earned vacation; and the only reason he'd phoned Sonia back was to borrow Rick's high-powered binoculars and a bird book about the West Indies. The book was now sitting in his lap, along with a list of the birds they were likely to see. He hadn't opened either one.

Why in God's name was he wasting two weeks of his precious time to go and see a woman who thought he was a liar and a cheat? A sexual cheat. How she'd laugh if she knew that somehow, in the eight months he and Gabrielle had been held for ransom in Colombia, Gabrielle had seemed more like the sister he'd never had, the mother he could only dimly remember, than a potential bed partner. This despite the fact that Gabrielle was a very attractive woman.

He'd never told Gabrielle that, and never would. Nor would he ever tell Rowan.

A man was entitled to his secrets.

Tension had pulled tight the muscles in Brant's neck and shoulders; he was aware of his heartbeat thin and high in his chest. But those weren't feelings, of course. They were just physiological reactions caused by adrenaline, fight or flight, a very useful mechanism that had gotten him out of trouble more times than he cared to count. The airplane was looking after the flight part, he thought semi-humorously. Which left fight.

Rowan would no doubt take care of that. She'd never been one to bite her tongue if she disagreed with him or disliked what he was doing; it was one of the reasons he'd married her, for the tilt of her chin and the defiant toss of her curly red hair.

Maybe she didn't care about him enough now to think him worth a good fight.

He didn't like that conclusion at all. With an impatient sigh Brant spread out the list of bird species and opened the book at page one, forcing himself to concentrate. After all, he didn't want to disgrace himself by not knowing one end of a bird from the other. Especially in front of his ex-wife.

Rowan could have done without the connecting flight from Antigua being four hours late. Rick Williams from Toronto was the last of her group to arrive: the only other Canadian besides herself on the trip. The delay seemed like a bad omen, because it was the second hitch of the day; she and the rest of the group had had an unexpected five hours of birding in Antigua already today when their Grenada flight had also been late.

Rick's flight should have landed in Grenada at six-thirty, in time for dinner with everyone else at the hotel. Instead it was now nearly ten forty-five and Rick still hadn't come through customs.

His luggage, she thought gloomily. They've lost his luggage.

She checked with the security guard and was allowed into the customs area. Four people were standing at the desk which dealt with lost bags. The elderly woman she discounted immediately, and ran her eyes over the three men. The gray-haired gentleman was out; Rick Williams was thirty-two years old. Which left…her heart sprang into her throat like a grouse leaping from the undergrowth. The man addressing the clerk was the image of Brant.

She swallowed hard and briefly closed her eyes. She was tired, yes, but not that tired.

But when she looked again, the man had straightened to his full height, his backpack pulling his blue cotton shirt taut across his shoulders. His narrow hips and long legs were clad in well-worn jeans. There was a dusting of gray in the thick dark hair over his ears. That was new, she thought numbly. He'd never had any gray in his hair when they'd been married.

It wasn't Brant. It couldn't be.

But then the man turned to say something to the younger man standing beside him, and she saw the imperious line of his jaw, shadowed with a day's dark beard, and the jut of his nose. It was Brant. Brant Curtis had turned up in the Grenada airport just as she was supposed to meet a member of one of her tours. Bad joke, she thought sickly, lousy coincidence, and dragged her gaze to the younger man. He must be Rick Williams.

Her eyes darted around the room. There was nowhere she could hide in the hopes that Brant would leave before Rick, and therefore wouldn't see her. She couldn't very well scuttle back through customs; they'd think she was losing her mind. Anyway, Rick was one of her clients, and she owed him whatever help she could give him if his bags were lost.

At least she'd had a bit of warning. She was exceedingly grateful for that, because she'd hate Brant to have seen all the shock and disbelief that must have been written large on her face in the last few moments; the harsh fluorescent lighting would have hidden none of it. Taking a deep breath, schooling her features to impassivity, Rowan walked toward the desk.

As if he'd sensed her presence Brant turned around, and for the first time in months she saw the piercing blue of his eyes, the blue of a desert sky. As they fastened themselves on her, not even the slightest trace of emotion crossed his face. Of course not, she thought savagely. He'd always been a master at hiding his feelings. It was one of the many things that had driven them apart, although he would never have acknowledged the fact. Rowan forced a smile to her lips and was fiercely proud that she sounded as impassive as he looked, "Well...what a surprise. Hello, Brant."

"What the devil have you done to your hair?"

Nearly three years since he'd seen her and all he could talk about was her hair? "I had it cut."

"For Pete's sake, what for?"

A small part of her was wickedly pleased that she'd managed to disrupt his composure; it had never been easy to knock Brant off balance, his self-control was too formidable for that. Rowan ran her fingers through her short, ruffled curls. "Because I wanted to. And now you must excuse me...I'm supposed to be meeting someone."

She turned to the younger man and said pleasantly, "You must be Rick Williams?"

The man glanced up from the form he was filling in; he smelled rather strongly of rum. "Nope. Sorry." Doing a double take, he looked her up and down. "Extremely sorry."

Rowan gritted her teeth. She rarely bothered with makeup on her tours, and her jeans and sport shirt were quite unexceptional. Why did men think that she could possibly be complimented when they eyed her like a specimen laid out on a tray? And where the heck was Rick Williams? If he'd missed the plane, why hadn't he phoned her?

Brant said, "Rick couldn't come. So I came in his place."

"*What?*"

"Rick has a form of pneumonia and the doctors wouldn't let him come," Brant repeated patiently. "It was all rather at the last minute, so I didn't bother letting you know."

She sputtered, "You knew if you let me know I wouldn't have let you come!"

"That's true enough," he said.

So that was why he hadn't looked surprised to see her; he'd known all along she'd be there to meet him. Once again, he'd had the advantage of her. "Were you bored and thought you'd stir up a little trouble?" she spat. "From reading the newspapers, I'd have thought there were more than enough wars and famines in the world to get your attention without having to turn yourself into an ordinary tourist in the Caribbean."

So she did care enough to fight, thought Brant. Interesting. Very interesting. He said blandly, "If we're going to have a—er, disagreement, don't you think we should at least go outside where there's a semblance of privacy?"

Rowan looked around her. The young man who wasn't Rick Williams was leering at her heaving chest; the customs officer was grinning at her. Trying to smother another uprush of pure rage, she managed, with a huge effort, to modulate her voice. "Is your baggage missing?"

Brant nodded. "They figure it's gone on to Trinidad— should be here tomorrow. No big deal."

"Have you finished filling in the forms?"

Another nod. "I'm ready to go anytime you are."

"I'll phone the airlines on the way out," she said crisply,

"and get you on the first flight back to Toronto. A birding trip is definitely not your thing."

"No, you won't. I've paid my money and I'm staying."

She'd forgotten how much taller he was than her five feet nine. How big he was. "Brant, let's not—"

He jerked his head at the door. "Outside. Not in here."

He was right, of course. Her company would fire her on the spot if it could see how she was greeting a client. She pivoted, stalked through the glass doors into the open part of the terminal and then out into the dusky heat of a tropical night. The van was parked by the curb. She swung herself into the driver's seat and took the key from the pocket of her jeans, shoving it into the ignition. Brant had climbed into the passenger seat. Turning to face him, Rowan said tautly, "So what's going on here?"

Brant took his time to answer. He was still getting used to her haircut, to that moment of outrage by the baggage counter when he'd realized she'd changed something about herself that he'd loved, changed it without asking him— and if that wasn't the height of irrationality he didn't know what was. The new haircut, he decided reluctantly, suited her, emphasizing the slim line of her throat and the exquisite angles of her cheekbones. Her eyes, a rich brown in daylight, now matched the velvety darkness of the sky. Eyes to drown in...

He said equably, "I needed a vacation. Through the friend of a friend I heard about Rick's pneumonia and thought I'd take his place. Don't make such a big deal of it, Rowan."

"If it's no big deal, why don't you just go home? Where you belong."

You don't belong with me, that's what she was saying. A statement that truly riled him. "You used to say—fairly frequently, as I recall—that I never took time to smell the roses. Or, in this case, to watch the birds...you should be pleased I'm finally doing so."

"Brant, let's get something straight. What you do or don't do is no longer my concern. Go watch the birds by all means. But don't do it on my turf."

"You've lost weight."

Her exasperated hiss of breath sounded very loud in the confines of the van. Brant watched her fight for composure, her knuckles gripping the steering wheel as if she were throttling him, and discovered to his amazement that he was enjoying himself. Enjoying himself? Was that why he'd come to Grenada?

To Rowan's nostrils drifted the faint tang of aftershave, the same one Brant had used during the four tempestuous years they'd been married. It brought with it a host of memories she didn't dare bring to the surface; she'd be lost if she did. Nevertheless, she let her eyes wander with a lazy and reckless intimacy down his flat belly. "You've lost weight, as well," she said and saw that, briefly, she'd stopped him in his tracks. "Am I right?" she added sweetly.

Brant glared at her in impotent fury. He knew exactly what was wrong. He wanted to kiss her. So badly that he could taste the soft yielding of her lips and the silken slide of her cheek, and feel the first stirring of his groin. But kissing Rowan wasn't part of the plan.

Not that he'd had a plan. He'd acted on impulse in a way rare to him, and now he was faced—literally—with the consequences. Rowan. His ex-wife. His former wife. His divorced wife.

His wife.

He said levelly, knowing he was backing off from something he should have anticipated and hadn't, "Look, it's been a long day and I'm tired. Please, could we go to the hotel so I can catch up on some sleep?''

"Certainly," she said. "But let me make something clear first. I'm doing my job in the next two weeks, Brant. A job I love and do well. You're just another client to me. Because I'm not going to allow you to be anything else— do you understand?''

"I haven't said I want to be anything else," he remarked, and watched her lips tighten.

"Good," she said viciously, and jammed the clutch into gear. The engine roared to life. She checked in the rearview mirror and pulled away from the curb.

Rowan was an excellent driver, and knew it; and she'd had the last twelve hours to get used to driving on the left. She whipped along the narrow streets, took the roundabout in fine style, and within fifteen minutes turned into the hotel, where she parked next to the rooms that were partway up the hill. "This is the only place we stay that isn't in close vicinity of a beach," she said, breaking a silence that to her, at least, had swarmed with things unsaid. "You're in Room Nine—Rick had requested a single room." She fished around in the little pack strapped to her waist. "Here's your key."

She was holding it in her fingertips. To test his immunity, Brant deliberately closed his hand over hers; and as soon as he'd done so, knew he'd made a very bad mistake. Her skin was warm and smooth, her fingers with that supple strength he'd never forgotten. But they were as still in his grip as a trapped bird, and when his glance flew to her face he saw in it a reflection of his own dismay. Dismay? Who was he kidding? It wasn't dismay. It was outright terror.

He snatched the key from her, its cool metal digging into his flesh. "What time do we get going in the morning?"

"Breakfast at six on the patio," she babbled, "but you

can sleep in if you want, there's a really nice beach about fifteen minutes from the hotel and you'd probably rather have a day to yourself to rest up.''

"I'll see you at six,'' he announced and got out of the van as fast as he could. Room Eight was in darkness. A small light shone from Room Ten. Then Rowan hurried past him, unlocked the patio door to Room Ten and shut it with rather more force than was necessary. He watched as she pulled the curtains tight over the glass.

Brant stood very still under the burgeoning yellow moon. Frogs chirped in the undergrowth; palm fronds were etched against the star-strewn night sky in a way that at any other time he might have found beautiful.

But palm trees weren't a priority right now. How could they be when his whole body was a raw ache of hunger? Sexual hunger. He wanted Rowan now, in his bed, in his arms, where she belonged...and to hell with the divorce. How was he going to get a minute's sleep, knowing she was on the other side of the wall from him?

He'd been a fool to come here, to let Gabrielle talk him into an escapade worthy of an adolescent. If he were smart he'd take Rowan's advice and get on the first plane home. Tomorrow.

Soft-footed, Brant walked over to his own door and inserted the key. The door opened smoothly. He closed it behind him, and heard the smallest of creaks from the room next to his. Rowan. Getting into bed. Did she still sleep naked?

He sat down on the wicker chair, banging his fists rhythmically on his knees. What kind of an idiot was he that he'd neglected to take into account the effect Rowan had had on him from the first time he'd ever seen her, arguing with a customs officer in the Toronto airport seven years ago? He'd engineered a conversation with her that day, had touched her wrist and had seen the instant flare of awareness in her face, the primitive recognition of female to male, of mate to mate. Would he ever forget how her pulse had leaped beneath his fingertip? That all-revealing signal had engraved itself on his flesh within five minutes of meeting her, and would probably remain with him as long as he lived.

Two days later they'd fallen into bed in his condo; three weeks later they were married. A month after that he'd left for Rwanda, and the fights between them had started, fights every bit as passionate as their ardent and imperative couplings.

Another tiny creak came from the room next door. He wanted to kick the wall in, gather her in his arms, make love to her the whole night through.

But this wasn't Myanmar or Afghanistan or Liberia. He couldn't bash his way into the next room. Rowan wasn't an arms smuggler or a drug dealer; she was his ex-wife.

How he hated that word! Almost as much as he hated the prospect, now almost a certainty, that he was in for one of his nights of insomnia, nights when too many of the nightmare images he usually kept at bay would crowd through his defenses, attacking him from every angle like an army of fanatic rebels.

Normally it took every bit of his strength and integrity to hold himself together during those nights; which were, fortunately, rare. Tonight he had the added, overwhelming torment of Rowan's presence on the other side of the wall. Would he ever forget the first time they'd made love? Her entrancing mixture of shyness and boldness, her astonishing generosity, her heart-catching beauty...he could remember every detail of that afternoon, which had blended into a night equally and wondrously passionate.

Brant buried his face in his hands, his back curved like a bow, a host of memories stabbing him like arrows.

CHAPTER TWO

ROWAN lay ramrod still in her double bed. The numbers of the digital alarm clock on the night table announced that it was 2:06. If she moved at all, the springs creaked. If she tossed and turned, sooner or later her elbow or her head thumped the wall. The wall that lay between her and Brant.

Her eyes ached. Her body twitched. Her nerves were singing as loudly as the frogs. And all the while her brain seethed with the knowledge that Brant was lying less than a foot away from her, separated from her by a thin barrier of stucco and plaster.

Separated from her by too many fights, too many angry words, too many long months of worrying about him and waiting for him, all the while trying to keep her own life on track. That last departure for Colombia had been, classically, the straw to break the back of their marriage. That and the woman called Gabrielle Doucette.

She had no idea how she was going to get through the next two weeks. No idea whatsoever.

2:09. She had to get some sleep. Tomorrow was a full day, although thank goodness she'd hired a driver and wouldn't have to negotiate roads that could be hair-raising at the best of times. Why *had* Brant come here? What stupidity had impelled him to seek her out just when she was beginning to hope that one day soon she might heal, that hovering somewhere on the horizon there was the possibility, however faint, of putting the past behind her and looking for a new relationship? One that would give her everything Brant had refused her.

How dare he interfere with her life, he who had damaged it so badly? How *dare* he?

Somewhere between two-thirty and quarter to three Rowan fell asleep as suddenly as if she'd been hit on the head. She woke sharp at 5:20; during the years she'd spent guiding tours, she'd trained herself to beat the alarm by ten minutes to give herself that space to think over the day ahead. As so often happened, everything seemed crystal clear to her now that it was morning.

She'd overreacted last night. Big time. And why not? It had been late at night. Her ex-husband had appeared totally unexpectedly and had thrown her for a loop. And again, why not? In all her thirty-one years he was the only man she'd ever fallen in love with; so she'd fallen in a major way. No holding back. No keeping part of herself for herself. She'd thrown herself into their relationship with passion, enthusiasm and a deep joy; and when, all too soon, rifts had appeared, she'd worked with all her heart to mend them. In consequence, the final and utter failure of their marriage had devastated her.

But that was a long time ago.

The only thing she'd have to beware of was touching him. The physical bond between them had never ruptured, not even in the worst of times, and when he'd wrapped his fingers around hers last night as she'd passed him the key, all the old magic had instantly exploded to life, like fireworks glittering against the blackness of sky.

He'd seduced her—literally—from the beginning. She mustn't, for her own sake, allow him to do it again.

There were six other people in the group; she'd have lots of protection. Plus the itinerary would keep everyone busy. On which note, Rowan thought lightly, you'd better get moving. She scrambled out of bed, headed for the shower and left her room at ten to six.

Breakfast started at six on a charming open patio twined with scarlet hibiscus and the yellow trumpet-shaped flowers called Allamanda. The six other members of the group were tucking into slices of juicy papaya; Brant was nowhere to be seen. Maybe he'd decided to heed her advice and take the day off, thought Rowan; or, even better, fly back to Toronto. She beamed at everyone, inquired how they'd all slept, and heard Brant's deep voice say from behind her, "Good morning—sorry I missed seeing all of you last night."

Rowan said evenly, "This is Brant Curtis, from Toronto. He's taking Rick's place, because Rick's ill with pneumonia." Quickly she introduced the others to Brant, then said, "I'm sure you won't remember everyone's name. But you'll soon get to know each other. Coffee, Brant?"

"Shower first, coffee second," he said easily, "that's been my routine for a long time."

He was smiling at her. Often they'd showered together; and they'd both loved Viennese coffee ground fresh and sweetened with maple syrup. Willing herself not to snarl at him, Rowan said, "Personally I prefer herbal tea—can't take the caffeine anymore."

Peg and May, the two elderly sisters from Dakota who looked fluttery and sweet and knew more about birds than most encyclopedias, passed Brant the plate of papaya and the cream for his coffee; Sheldon and Karen, the newlyweds from Maine, gave him the bemused smiles they gave everything and everyone; Steve and Natalie, unmarried and so argumentative that Rowan sincerely hoped they weren't contemplating marriage, both eyed Brant speculatively. Steve no doubt saw Brant as a potential rival for Alpha male; whereas Natalie was probably wanting to haul him off to bed the minute Steve was looking the other way.

Brant was a big boy. Let Brant deal with Natalie.

Peg said, "You missed some wonderful shorebirds in Antigua yesterday, Brant. But you'll have lots of time to catch up...I'm sure you saw the mangrove cuckoo in the breadfruit tree?"

"And the black form of the bananaquit in the bougain-villea?" May added.

Brant took a deep draft of coffee; he was going to need it. He said cautiously, dredging his memory for the pictures in the bird book, "I thought a bananaquit was yellow?" and realized he'd said exactly the right thing. Peg and May launched into an enthusiastic and mystifying discussion about isolation and Darwinian theory, to which he nodded and looked as though he understood every word, munching all the while on a deliciously crumbly croissant smothered with jam.

Natalie, who was wearing a cotton shirt with rather a lot of buttons undone, smoothed her sleek black hair back from her face and pouted her fuschia-colored lips at him. "On the way back to our rooms, Brant, I'll have to show you where I saw the crested hummingbird."

"You can show me first," Steve said aggressively; he had the build of a wrestler and the buzzed haircut of a marine.

"Oh," piped Karen, who had fluffy blond curls and art-less blue eyes, "what's that black bird with the long tail on the ledge of the patio?"

"A male Carib grackle," Rowan replied. "The equiva-lent of our starling, we'll be seeing a lot of them."

Sheldon, Karen's husband, said nothing; he was too busy gazing at Karen in adoration.

Everyone else, Brant saw, had brought binoculars to the table; he'd forgotten his. Rowan looked as though she hadn't had much more sleep than he'd had. Good, he thought meanly, and took another croissant. He was already beginning to realize that keeping up with this lot was going to take a fair bit of energy and that he probably should have read more of the bird book and thought less about Rowan on the long flight from Toronto.

Not that he was here to see birds.

He was here to see Rowan—right?

By the time they left the hotel, the sky had clouded over and rain was spattering the windshield. Their first stop was an unprepossessing stretch of scrubby forest on the side of a hillside, the residence of an endangered species called the Grenada dove. Brant trooped with the rest up the slope, thorns snatching at his shirt and bare wrists, rain dripping down his neck. Wasn't April supposed to be the dry season? Where was the famous sunshine of the Caribbean? Where were the white sand beaches? And why was Rowan way ahead of him and he last in line? Natalie, not to his surprise, was directly in front of him, an expensive camera looped over her shoulder, her hips undulating like a model's on a catwalk. He'd met plenty of Natalies over the years, and avoided them like the plague; especially when they were teamed with bruisers like Steve.

When they were all thoroughly enmeshed in the forest, Rowan took out a tape deck and played a recording of the dove, its mournful cooing not improving Brant's mood. She was intent on what she was doing, her eyes searching the forest floor, all her senses alert. Maybe if he blatted like a dove she'd notice he was here, he thought sourly.

They all trudged further up the hillside and she played the tape again; then moved to another spot, where there was a small clearing. Rowan replayed the tape. From higher up the slope a soft, plangent cooing came in reply. She whispered, "Hear that? Check out that patch of under-growth by the gumbo-limbo tree."

Brant didn't know a gumbo-limbo tree from a coconut palm. Peg said, "Oh, there's the dove! Do you see it, May? Working its way between the thorn bushes."

"I can see it," Natalie remarked. "Not sure I can get a photo, though."

"Then why can't I find it?" Steve fumed.

"Come over here, Steve," Rowan said, "I've got it in the scope."

She'd been carrying a large telescope on a tripod; Brant watched Steve stoop to look in the eyepiece. Then Karen and Sheldon peered in. Rowan said, "Look for the white shoulders and the white patch on the head. Brant, have you seen it?"

He hadn't. Obediently he walked over and looked through the lens, seeing a dull brown pigeon with a crescent of white on its side. Natalie rubbed against him with her hip. "My turn, Brant," she murmured.

May—who had mauve-rinsed hair while Peg had blue—said to him, "Isn't that a *wonderful* bird?"

She was grinning from ear to ear; Brant couldn't possibly have spoiled her pleasure. "A terrific bird," he said solemnly.

Ten minutes later they emerged back into the cleared land at the base of the scrub forest, and Rowan swept the area with her binoculars. Then she gasped in amazement. "Look—near the papaya tree. A pair of them!"

Brant raised his binoculars. Two more doves were pecking at the earth, their white markings clearly visible. Peg and May sighed with deep satisfaction, Natalie adjusted her zoom lens for a picture and Rowan said exultantly, "This is one of the rarest birds of the whole trip and we've seen three of them! I can't believe it."

Instead of staring at the doves, Brant stared at Rowan. Her cheeks were flushed, her face alight with pleasure; she used to look that way when he'd walked in the door after a three-week absence, he thought painfully. Or after they'd made love.

She glanced up, caught his fixed gaze on her and narrowed her eyes, closing him out; her chin was raised, her damp curls like tiny flames. Steve snapped, "Hurry up and put the scope on them, Rowan."

Rowan gave a tiny start. "Sorry," she said, and lowered the tripod.

Don't you talk to my wife like that.

His own words, which had been entirely instinctive, played themselves in Brant's head like one of Rowan's tapes. She wasn't his wife. Not anymore. And why should it matter to him how a jerk like Steve behaved? Furious with himself, he raised his glasses and watched the two doves work their way along a clump of bushes.

Then Peg said, "A pair of blue-black grassquits at the edge of the sugarcane," and everyone's binoculars, with the exception of Brant's, swiveled to the left.

"How beautiful," May sighed.

"This is the only island we'll see them," Peg added.

"Take a look in the scope, Karen," Rowan offered.

They all lined up for a turn. Brant was last. "All I can see is sugarcane," he said.

Quickly Rowan edged him aside, adjusting the black levers. Her left hand was bare of rings, he saw with a nasty flick of pain, as if a knife had scored his bare skin. "There they are, they'd moved," she said, and backed away.

Into his vision leaped a small glossy bird and its much duller mate. A pair, he thought numbly, and suddenly wished with all his heart that he was back in his condo in Toronto, or striding along the bustling streets of Yangon, Myanmar's capital city. Anything would be better than having Rowan so close and yet so unutterably far away.

They tramped back to the van, adding several other birds to the list on the way, all of whose names Brant forgot as soon as they were mentioned. He couldn't sit beside Rowan; she was in the front with the driver. He took the jump seat next to Peg and tried to listen to the tale of habitat destruction that had made the dove such a rarity.

They drove north next, to the rain forests in the center of the island, where dutifully Brant took note of humming-birds, tanagers, swifts, flycatchers and more bananaquits. Not even the sight of a troop of Mona monkeys cavorting in a bamboo grove could raise his spirits. His mood was more allied to the thunderclouds hovering on the horizon, a mood as black-hearted as the black-feathered and omni-present grackles.

When they reached some picnic tables by a murky lake, Rowan busied herself laying out paper plates and cutlery, producing drinks and a delicious pasta salad from a cooler, as well as crusty rolls, fruit and cookies out of various bags. She did all this with a cheerful efficiency that grated on Brant's nerves. How could she be so happy when he felt like the pits? How could she joke with a macho idiot like Steve?

He sat a little apart from the rest of the group, feeding a fair bit of his lunch to a stray dog that hovered nearby. He had considerable fellow feeling for it; however, Rowan wasn't into throwing him anything, not even the smallest of scraps. To her he was just one more member of the group; she'd make sure he saw the birds and got fed and that was where her responsibility ended.

He felt like a little kid exiled from the playground. He felt like a grown man with a lump in his gut bigger than a crusty roll and ten times less digestible. He fed the last of his roll to the dog and buried his nose in the bird book, trying to sort out bananaquits from grassquits.

Their next destination was a mangrove swamp at the northern tip of the island. Although it had stopped raining, the sweep of beach and the crash of waves seemed to increase Brant's sense of alienation.

Rowan glanced around. "The trail circling the swamp is at the far end of those palm trees."

"I'm going to wait here," Brant said. "I can see the van, so I'll know when you get back."

"Suit yourself," she said with an indifferent shrug.

May protested, "But you might miss the egrets."

"Or the stilts," Peg said.

"I'm going for a swim," Brant said firmly.

May brightened. "Maybe you'll see a tropic bird."

He didn't know a tropic bird from a gull; but he didn't tell her that. "Maybe I will."

"I wish you'd told us this morning we'd be at a beach, Rowan," Natalie said crossly. "I'd love a swim."

"You came here to photograph birds," Steve announced, and grabbed her by the wrist. She glared at him and he glared right back.

"We'd better go," Rowan said quickly. "Once we've trekked around the swamp we have a long drive home."

Brant had put on his trunks under his jeans that morning; he left his gear with the driver of the van, shucked off his clothes and ran into the water, feeling the waves seize him in their rough embrace. He swam back and forth in the surf as fast as he could, blanking from his mind everything but the salt sting of the sea and the pull of his muscles. When he finally looked up, the group was trailing along the beach toward him.

He hauled himself out of the waves, picked up his clothes from the sand and swiped at his face with his towel. Rowan was first in line. He jogged over to her, draping his towel over his shoulder. "Did I miss the rarest egret in the world?"

Midafternoon had always been the low point of the day for Rowan; and the sight of Brant running across the sand toward her in the briefest of swim trunks wasn't calculated to improve her mood. She said coldly, staring straight ahead, "There was a white-tailed tropic bird flying right over your head."

"No kidding."

She hated the mockery in his voice, hated his closeness even more. Then his elbow bumped her arm. "Sorry," he said.

He wasn't sorry; she knew darn well he'd done it on purpose. But Peg and May were right behind her and she couldn't possibly let loose the flood of words that was crowding her tongue. She bit her lip, her eyes skidding sideways of their own accord. The sunlight was glinting on the water that trickled down Brant's ribs and through the dark hair that curled on his chest. His belly was as flat as a board, corded with muscle; she didn't dare look lower.

To her infinite relief a night heron flew over the trees. Grabbing her binoculars, Rowan blanked from her mind the image of Brant's sleek shoulders and taut ribs. He meant nothing to her now. Nothing. She had to hold to that thought or she'd be sunk.

The yellow-crowned night heron was obliging enough to settle itself in the treetops, where it wobbled rather endearingly in the wind. Karen had never seen one before. Quickly Rowan set up the scope, immersing herself in her job again, and when next she looked Brant was standing by the van fully clothed.

Thank God for small mercies, she thought, and shepherded her little flock back into the van. On the drive home along the coast she gave herself a stern lecture about keeping her cool when she was anywhere in Brant's vicinity, whether he was clothed or unclothed. She couldn't bear for him to know that the sight of his big rangy body had set her heart thumping in her breast like a partridge drumming on a tree stump in mating season.

It was none of his business. He'd lost any right to know her true feelings; he'd trampled on them far too often.

He was a client of the company she worked for, one more client on one more trip.

Maybe if she repeated this often enough, she'd start to believe it. Maybe.

CHAPTER THREE

AT DINNER Brant ate curried chicken and mango ice cream as though they were so much cardboard, and tried to talk to Karen, whose sole topic of conversation was Sheldon, rather than to Natalie, whose every topic was laced with sexual innuendo. Rowan was sitting at the other end of the table laughing and chatting with Steve, May and Peg; she looked carefree and confident. He had the beginnings of a headache.

Would he be a coward to fly back to Toronto? Or was it called common sense instead?

People dispersed after dinner; it was nine-fifty and they had to be up before six to leave for the airport, to fly to the next island on the itinerary. Rowan had already gone to her room. Brant found himself standing outside her patio doors, where, once again, the curtains were drawn tight. Without stopping to consider what he was doing, let alone why, he raised his fist, tapped on the glass, and in a voice that emulated Steve's gravelly bass he said, "Rowan? Steve here. Do you have any Tylenol? Natalie's got a headache."

"Just a second," she called.

Then the door opened and at the same instant that her eyes widened in shock, Brant shoved his foot in the gap and pushed it still wider, wide enough that he could step through. Rowan said in a furious whisper, "Brant, get out of here!"

He closed the door behind him. She had started undressing; her feet were bare and her shirt pulled out of her waistband, the top two buttons undone. In the soft lamplight her skin looked creamy and her hair glowed like a banked fire.

She spat, "Go away and leave me alone—you're good at doing that, you've had lots of practice."

"For God's sake, leave the past out of this!"

"I despise you for pulling a trick like that, pretending you were Steve. Although it's just what I should expect from someone so little in tune with his feelings, so removed from—"

Brant had had enough. With explosive energy he said, "I'm not leaving until you tell me how else I'm going to get five minutes alone with you."

"I don't want ten seconds alone with you!"

"We're not going to spend the next two weeks pretending I've come all this way just to see a bunch of dumpy old pigeons."

Rowan felt her body freeze to stillness; in the midst of that stillness she remembered the resolve she'd made in the van. To keep her cool, her feelings hidden. She wasn't doing very well in that department so far; she'd better see what she could do to improve matters. Forcing herself to lower her voice, she said, "So why not tell me why you've come here, Brant?"

He gaped at her. *Because Gabrielle told me to?* That would go over like a lead balloon. "I just wanted to see you," he said lamely.

"You've seen me," she replied without a trace of emotion. "Now you can go back to Toronto. Or to whatever benighted part of the globe you're writing about next. Either way, I want you to stay away from me."

"Don't I mean anything to you anymore?"

He hadn't meant to say that. Her lips thinned. She answered tersely, "If you're asking if I'll ever forget you, the answer's probably no—the damage went too deep for that.

If you're asking if I want to revive any kind of a relationship with you, the answer's absolutely no. And for the very same reason.''

''You've changed.''

''I would hope so.''

''I didn't mean it as a compliment! You never used to be so cold. So hard.''

''Then you can congratulate yourself on what you've accomplished.''

''You never used to be bitchy, either,'' he retorted, his temper rising in direct proportion to his need to puncture her self-possession.

''I'd call it a good dose of the truth rather than bitchiness. But there's no reason we should agree on that, we never agreed on anything else.'' Suddenly Rowan ran her fingers through her cropped hair, her pent-up breath escaping in a long sigh. ''This is really stupid, standing here trading insults with each other. It's been a long day and I've got to be up at five-thirty. So I'm just going to say one more thing, Brant, then I want you to leave. I made a mistake seven years ago when I married you. I've paid for that mistake—it cost me plenty. And now I'm moving on. For all kinds of obvious reasons I don't need your help to do that. Get yourself on the first plane back to Toronto and kindly stay out of my life.''

Her fists were clenched at her sides and she was very pale. The woman Brant had been married to would have been yelling at him by now, passion exuding from every pore, her words pouring out as clamorously as a waterfall tumbles over a cliff. Had she really changed that much? Even worse, was he, as she'd said, responsible for that change?

Rowan picked up the receiver of the phone by her bed,

knowing she had to end this. "I'll give you ten seconds. Then I'm calling the front desk."

"Go right ahead," he drawled. "I'll make sure I tell them I'm your ex-husband. I'll tell Natalie, too—she'll spread the word to the group, I'm sure."

"You wouldn't!"

He bared his teeth in a smile. "I've never been known for fighting fair. Had you forgotten?"

She hadn't. One of his weapons had always been his body, of course; his body and the searing sexual bond between the two of them. Suddenly frightened, Rowan said, "Brant, don't do this. You're only making things worse between us."

"According to you, that's impossible."

She took another deep breath and said steadily, "I can only speak for myself here. I still have some good memories—some wonderful memories—of the time we spent together. But when you force your way into my room like this, and threaten to expose my private life to a group of strangers who happen to be my business clients, then I start to wonder if I'm kidding myself about those memories—I was deluded, I wasn't seeing the real man, he never existed. Don't do that to me, Brant. Please."

Some of the old intensity was back in her voice, and there was no doubting her sincerity. Shaken, in spite of himself, Brant blurted, "Is there someone else in your life, Rowan?"

"No," she said flatly. "But I want there to be."

Relief, rage and chagrin battled in his chest: he'd never meant to ask that question. Where the devil was his famous discretion, his ability to control a conversation and learn exactly what he wanted to know from someone who'd had no intention of revealing it? His boss would fire him if he could see him in action right now. Defeated by a woman? Brant Curtis?

He said thickly, "One kiss. For old time's sake."

Panic flared in her face. She grabbed the phone and cried, "You come one step nearer and I'll tell everyone in Grenada that you're the world-famous journalist, Michael Barton. So help me, I will."

Michael Barton was Brant's pseudonym, and only a very small handful of people knew that Brant Curtis and Michael Barton were one and the same man; it was this closely guarded secret that enabled him as Brant Curtis, civil engineer and skilled negotiator, to enter with impunity whichever country he was investigating. He felt an ill-timed flare of admiration for Rowan; it was quite clear that she'd do it, she whom he'd trusted for years with his double identity.

"You sure don't want me to kiss you, do you?" he jeered. "Why not, Rowan? Afraid we'll end up in bed?"

"Look up divorce in the dictionary, why don't you? We're through, finished, kaput. I wouldn't go to bed with you if you were the last man on earth."

"Bad cliché, my darling."

With a huge effort Rowan prevented herself from throwing the telephone at him, cord and all. Keep your cool, Rowan. Keep your cool. She said evenly, "It happens to be true."

"But why so adamant? Who are you trying to convince?"

She said with a sudden, corrosive bitterness, "The one man in the world who never allowed himself to be convinced of anything I said."

She meant it, Brant thought blankly. Her bitterness was real, laden with a pain whose depths horrified him. He stood very still, at a total loss for words. He earned his living—an extraordinarily good living—by words. Yet right now he couldn't find anything to say to the woman who had been his lover and his wife. She looked exhausted, he realized with a pang of what could only be compassion, her shoulders slumped, her cheeks pale as the stuccoed walls.

As if she had read his mind, she said in a low voice, "Brant, I work fifteen-hour days for two weeks on this trip and I've got to get some sleep."

"Yeah...I'm sorry," he muttered, and headed for the door. Sorry for what? For bursting into her room? Or for killing the fieriness in her spirit all those months ago?

Was her accusation true? Had he never allowed her to change his mind about anything? If so, no wonder she wouldn't give him the time of day.

The door slid smoothly open and shut just as smoothly. He didn't once look back. Instead of going to his own room, he tramped down the driveway and left the hotel grounds. He'd noticed a bar not that far down the road. He'd order a double rum and hope it would make him sleep. Or six of them in a row. And he wouldn't allow his own good memories—of which there were many— to come to the surface.

He'd be done in if he did.

The patio door closed. As though she couldn't help herself, Rowan peered through the gap in the curtain and watched Brant's tall figure march down the driveway, until it blended with the darkness and disappeared. Shivering, she clicked the lock and pulled the curtain tightly shut. After dragging off the rest of her clothes, she pulled on silk pajamas and got into bed, yanking the covers over her head.

What would have happened if Brant had kissed her? Would he be lying beside her now, igniting her body to passion as only he could?

She slammed on her mental brakes, for to follow that

thought was to invite disaster. She hadn't let him kiss her. She'd kept some kind of control over herself and over him, in a way that was new. Dimly she felt rather proud of this.

Perhaps, she thought with a flare of hope, something good would come out of Brant's reappearance in her life. Perhaps there was a reason for it, after all. Inadvertently she'd been given an opportunity to lay the ghosts of the past to rest. If she could detach herself from him in the next two weeks, really detach herself, then when she went home she'd be free of him. Free to start over and find someone else.

She wanted children, and a man with a normal job. She wanted stability and continuity and a house in the country. She wanted to love and be loved.

By someone safe. Not by Brant with his restless spirit and his inexhaustible appetite for danger. Never again by a man like Brant.

Freedom, she thought, and closed her eyes. Freedom...

At the St. Vincent airport, while he was waiting to go through customs, Brant phoned three different airlines to see if he could get back to Toronto. It was nearing the end of the season, he was told; bookings were heavy. He could go standby. He could be rerouted in various complicated and extremely expensive ways. But he couldn't get on a plane today and end up in Toronto by nightfall.

He banged down the phone and took his passport out. When he rejoined the group he saw that he wasn't the only one to have left it. Natalie and Steve were standing to one side. Natalie was, very nearly, screaming; Steve was, unquestionably, yelling. Their language made Brant wince, their mutual fury made him glance at Rowan. She was talking to May and Peg, a fixed smile on her face.

Then Natalie stomped over to Rowan. Not bothering to

lower her voice, her catlike beauty distorted by rage, she announced, "Get me a single room for the rest of this trip! I'm not going anywhere near that—" and here her language, once again, achieved gutter level.

May said crisply, "Young woman, that's enough!"

Peg added, "This is a public place on a foreign island and you're disgracing our country."

Natalie's head swerved. "Who the hell do—"

"Be quiet," Peg ordered.

"This minute," her cohort seconded.

As Natalie's jaw dropped, Brant threw back his head and started to laugh, great bellows of laughter that released the tension in his chest and the ache in his belly that had been with him ever since he'd first seen Rowan in the airport at Grenada. Uncertainly Karen smiled and Sheldon joined her; a smile tugged at the corner of Rowan's mouth and Steve said vengefully, "Shut up, Natalie."

For a moment it looked as though Natalie was about to launch into another tirade. But then the custom's officer said, "Next, please," and Rowan said briskly, "Your turn, Natalie."

As Natalie stepped over the painted line and fumbled for her passport, Steve said, "Two single rooms, Rowan, and it's the last time I'll travel anywhere with that b—" he caught sight of May's clamped jaw and finished hastily "—broad."

"I'll do my best," Rowan said.

"You'd better," said Steve.

"There's a marvelous word in the English language, Steve, called please," Brant interposed softly. "You might try it sometime. Because I don't like it when you order Rowan around."

Steve took a step toward him, his fists bunched. Even

more softly, Brant said, "Don't do it. You'll end up flat on the floor seeing a lot more than birds."

This whole trip was getting away from her, Rowan thought wildly. A screaming match in the airport and now the threat of a brawl. But, try as she might, she couldn't take her eyes off Brant. Once, she remembered, she and he had been walking down Yonge Street and had been accosted by a couple of teenagers with knives; that evening Brant had had the same air of understated menace, of a lean and altogether dangerous confidence in his ability to defend both himself and her.

It wasn't his job to defend her. Not anymore. Besides which, dammit, it was time she asserted her own authority. "I've said I'll do my best, Steve, that's all I can do," she announced. "And you'll both have to pay extra money, you do realize that? Karen and Sheldon, why don't you go through customs next?" That, at least, would keep Natalie and Steve apart. She'd have to get on the phone at the hotel in St. Vincent and rearrange all the other hotels. And if Steve and Natalie had a reconciliation before the end of the trip, they could darn well sleep apart. It would be good for them.

Not entirely by coincidence, she glanced at Brant. He was watching her, laughter gleaming anew in his blue eyes. It's not funny, she told herself, and winked at him, her lips twitching; then suddenly remembered she was supposed to be keeping her cool. What a joke! How could she possibly keep her cool with Natalie and Steve fighting like alley cats, Peg and May acting like the imperious headmistresses of the very snootiest of private schools, and Karen and Sheldon looking superior because they knew they'd never do anything so crude as to argue?

Not to mention Brant. Handsome, sexy, irresistible Brant. She looked away, flustered and upset. Deep down she could admit to herself that she was extremely gratified Brant had sprung to her defense. And explain that one, Rowan Carter.

The hotel in St. Vincent boasted enough bougainvillea and palm trees for any postcard, as well as a dining room open to a view of the beach and a bar with pleasant wicker furniture right at the edge of the beige-colored sand. Rowan was able to get Steve and Natalie single rooms in separate wings of the hotel, and suggested they all meet for an early lunch. She then had the baggage delivered to all the right rooms, got on the phone to the rest of the hotels, and did some groceries for the picnic lunch the next day. By which time she was supposed to be in the dining room.

Steve sat down on one side of her, Brant on the other. Natalie, she saw with an unholy quiver of amusement, immediately seized the chair on Brant's far side. Okay, Rowan, she told herself, this time you really are going to keep your cool, and said brightly, "This afternoon we'll head up to the rain forest, where we should see St. Vincent parrots."

"Excellent," said May.

"Exciting," said Peg.

Steve nudged Rowan with something less than subtlety. "I'll stand you a drink in the bar for every parrot we see."

Over my dead body, thought Brant.

"I don't think so," Rowan responded. "We saw well over a dozen on our last trip here."

"Steve excels at drinking too much, it's his only talent," Natalie said sweetly. "I bet you can hold your liquor, Brant."

"So much so that I have no need to prove it," Brant replied. "Rowan, how long a drive to the forest?"

He was smiling at her, his irises the deep blue of the sea,

his dark hair ruffled by the breeze that came from the sea. We're divorced, Rowan thought frantically, we're finished, we're over and done with, and gulped, "Oh, about an hour, depending if we stop on the way."

"The St. Vincent parrots are the ones with yellow and blue on them."

"That's right, although it's more like gold and bronze, along with blue, green and white."

"You look tired," he said quietly.

She was tired. Her period was due soon, and she knew she'd have to dose herself with medication to get through the cramps on the first day. She said in a loud voice, "Because they're such handsome birds, they've been poached a lot for the parrot trade."

This launched Peg and May into a discussion about the complexities of economics and environmentalism, and thankfully Rowan focused on her conch salad. When they'd all finished eating, she asked everyone to meet in the lobby in fifteen minutes, and scurried off to ask the kitchen if they'd cook some tortellini for the picnic lunch the next day.

The others went to their rooms. Brant filled his canteen with water from the table, enjoying the breeze, remembering how the skin beneath Rowan's dark eyes was shadowed blue. He'd never before considered how hard she worked; her job had always seemed like a piece of cake compared to his. Not really worth his attention.

This wasn't a particularly comfortable thought. His eyes fell to her chair; she'd left her haversack there. When he bent to pick it up so he could return it to her, he discovered that it was astonishingly heavy. Without stopping to think, he slid the zipper open and looked inside.

What for? Photos of himself? That was a laugh. Photos of another man? That wouldn't be one bit funny.

She wasn't dating anyone else. She'd told him so. And in all the years he'd known Rowan, she'd never lied to him.

Brant was highly skilled at swift searches. The weight of the haversack was due to binoculars, a camera and a zoom lens. No photos turned up. But in a pocket deep in a back compartment he found something that made his pulses lurch, then thrum in his ears. His fingers were caressing the cool ceramic surface of the earrings he'd had designed for her, earrings fashioned like the berries of the rowan tree.

"*What* are you doing?"

Like a little boy caught with his hand in the cookie jar, Brant looked up. He fumbled for the earrings and held them up. "These were the first present I ever gave you."

She whispered ferociously, "You're on vacation, Brant—but you can't give it a rest, can you? You've always got to be the perfect investigator, the one who invades and violates the privacy of others for your own ends. Why don't you just lay off?"

"Why were these earrings buried in your haversack?"

"That's none of your damned business!"

She was swearing at him, he thought in deep relief; the ice-cold, controlled woman of last night was gone. In her place was a woman whose eyes blazed, whose cheeks were stained red with rage and whose breasts—those delectable breasts—were heaving. He retorted, "Just answer the question."

"Oh, because I'm dying with love for you," she stormed. "I'm obsessed with you, I think about you night and day, week in, week out. Hadn't you guessed that? Or could it just possibly be because I'd planned to wear them on this trip since they're kind of neat earrings and when you arrived I decided against it, in case I put any ideas in your head?" She snorted. "I don't need to put any ideas in your head, you can come up with more than enough all by yourself.''

''I didn't—''

''I'm actually starting to be pleased that you're here, Brant Curtis, and how do you feel about that? Do you know why?'' She didn't stop long enough for him to answer. ''You're confirming all the reasons I left you. Every last one of them. By the time you get on the plane in Antigua to go home, I'll be free as a—as a bird, and don't you dare tell me that's another cliché. I'm going to get on with my life. Without you. And I'm beginning to think I'll have you to thank for that.''

So angry he was beyond thought, Brant closed the distance between them in two long strides. Taking her furious face in his hands, the earrings digging into her cheek, he planted a kiss full on her open mouth.

Rowan kicked out at him; his tongue sought all the sweetness he'd missed so desperately for so long, and from behind them Peg gasped, ''Oh, my goodness!''

Brant dropped his hands as if they were clasping fire. Rowan, he noticed distantly, looked as though she might fall down. May said, ''Well, this is a surprise.''

Briefly Rowan closed her eyes in horror, wishing she could open them and find herself anywhere but in the dining room of the Beachside Hotel on the island of St. Vincent. Then she turned around. Peg and May were the only members of the group to be present, for which she thanked her lucky stars. Before she could think of what to say next, Brant said, ''We—er, we knew each other. From before. Rowan and I.''

He sounded as off balance as she felt. ''Yes,'' she faltered, ''that's right. From before. In—in Toronto.''

Somewhere she'd read that if you were going to lie, it

was best to stay as close to the truth as possible. "A couple
of years ago," she added.

"We'd rather you didn't tell the rest of them," Brant
said.

"Much rather," Rowan gulped. It was odd to feel herself
allied with Brant, even temporarily like this. Very odd.

"Just so long as you behave yourself, young man," May
said severely. "I've been on six different trips with Rowan
and she's one of the best."

"Yes, ma'am," Brant said. He'd had a teacher in grade
five of whom he'd been healthily in awe; May and Peg,
separately and collectively, fostered in him much the same
feeling.

"*The* best," Peg corroborated.

"I'd better get my binoculars," Brant said hastily,
dropped the earrings into Rowan's palm and fled.

Fight or flight? If it was Peg and May, he'd choose flight
any day, he thought, unlocking the door to his room. But
if it was Rowan?

Rowan was glad he was here because it was enabling
her to free herself from him.

He didn't like that one bit. In fact, he hated it with every
fiber of his being. So what was he going to do about it?
Fight? Or run away? The choice was his.

As he brushed his teeth, something else clicked into his
brain. Normally, strategy was an integral part of his life.
Before he left on any of his assignments, he researched the
area exhaustively, planned his itinerary and tried to antici-
pate all the things that could go wrong. Quite often, his life
had depended on this.

Ever since Gabrielle had shown him the brochure for this
trip, he'd been acting like a stray bullet ricocheting between
two cliffs. Fighting with Rowan at the Grenada airport.

Forcing his way into her room. Searching her bag. Kissing her in a public dining room.

Only a couple of months ago a reviewer, referring to one of his articles, had spoken of his cool, multifaceted intelligence. Maybe it was time he tried to resurrect that intelligence.

Maybe his life depended on it.

Startled, Brant stared at himself in the mirror over the sink. Did it? Is that why he was here?

Then he caught sight of his watch. He was going to be late. Grabbing his haversack and binoculars from the bed, he left the room. But one thing was clear to him. He needed to kiss Rowan again. In privacy and taking his time. He had to know if she'd respond to him. Because if she did, she couldn't very well move on to another man.

No, sirree.

CHAPTER FOUR

THE road to the St. Vincent rain forest grew narrower and narrower, winding along sharp drops without a trace of a guardrail, passing through little villages where goats and donkeys watched the van pass by, and uniformed school-children waved at its occupants. Finally they reached a small parking lot, and everyone clambered out.

Rowan loved this particular nature reserve. The volcanic mountains, green-clad, reared themselves against the sky. Puffy white clouds were sailing along in the wind, which hissed through the sabered fronds of palms and rattled the broad leaves of the banana trees. Cows grazed at the boundary of the reserve, accompanied by white-plumed cattle egrets. She led the way up the slope, passing the picnic area where they'd eat lunch the next day. She had lots of time to find the birds and she felt much better for having told Brant a few home truths.

Freedom to get on with her life. Not until she'd put that into words had she realized the extent to which she'd been on hold the last two years. She'd been a walking zombie. A woman uninterested in other men, bored or repelled by her few attempts at dating, her sexuality buried as deeply as her emotions.

Time for a change, she thought blithely, and when Steve offered to carry the scope, accepted with a smile that was perhaps more friendly than was wise.

Brant saw that smile. He clenched his jaw, feeling a primitive upsurge of male possessiveness; he'd long ago concluded that civilization could be a very thin skin over instincts and urges that ran far more deeply and imperatively.

Which led to the one question he was very determinedly ignoring. The question of whether he still loved Rowan.

She brought the group to a halt in an open area, and within minutes they were rewarded by a pair of birds flapping rapidly across their field of vision. Brant would never have known them for parrots; they were too far away. But parrots they apparently were.

Unimpressed, he brought up the rear as they entered the dense shadows of the rain forest. A stream ran alongside the trail; tree ferns waved their delicate fronds above his head, and bamboos whispered gently in the breeze; the vertical strands of lianas dropped from the heights of balsa trees to the ground, like the bars of a cage. He'd spent a lot of time in rain forests over the years, in the golden triangle of Thailand, in Myanmar and Borneo and Papua New Guinea. He trudged along, answering Natalie's attempts at conversation with minimal politeness.

The first flurry of excitement was a cocoa thrush; they hadn't sighted one in Grenada, so St. Vincent was their last chance. It was a chubby brown bird of no particular distinction, in Brant's opinion nothing to get excited about. The same was true of the next sighting, a whistling warbler endemic to St. Vincent. He caught a glimpse high in the canopy of a black and white bird, and in the scope saw the dark band across its chest that the bird book depicted. Rowan, Peg and May were beaming; although she couldn't get a photo of the warbler, even Natalie temporarily forgot him in its favor.

The pace was excruciatingly slow. He dropped back for a while, not wanting to talk to anyone, watching the small patches of sunlight waver through the trees, noticing how everything green struggled toward that light. Every other time he'd been in rain forests, his nerves had been stretched tight, alert for dangers that ranged from drug gangs to rebel guerrillas. There was no danger today. No reason why he shouldn't stop to admire a fern's single-minded climb up the trunk of a waterwood tree, or listen to the innocent burble of the stream in its mossy bed. He began to pick out individual birdcalls; he watched a black and scarlet ant lug a scrap of leaf across the path.

A flicker of movement in the trees caught his attention. When he raised his binoculars, he saw a most peculiar brown and white bird that was fluttering its wings continually, a big, smooth-feathered bird with a predatory bill. A trembler, he thought, remembering his reading on the plane, and flicked through the bird book until he found it. Feeling very pleased with himself for actually having identified something, he caught up with the rest of them.

"You missed the brown trembler," Natalie chided.

"No, I didn't," he said, and grinned at Rowan.

"Have you seen the tanager?" she asked, pointing to the scope. "Lesser Antillean tanager, St. Vincent race."

Brant gazed into the eyepiece. Into his field of vision leaped a bird with jade wings, a bronze cap and a rich, golden back, all its feathers gleaming as though they had been polished especially for him. He raised his head, looked straight at Rowan and said huskily, "It's very beautiful. Its head's the same color as your hair."

She blushed fierily. Steve pushed him aside, growling, "Let me have a look."

That remark hadn't been part of Brant's strategy. But it had worked. If she was ready to move on to someone else, why should a compliment from him so evidently discompose her?

The next bird they sighted was a solitaire, a handsome bird with gray, white and rufous plumage, whose clear, chiming call sounded as ethereal as a boys' choir in a ca-thedral. Rowan then located a ruddy quail dove, followed by a purple-throated Carib. The Carib, so Brant discovered, was a hummingbird. At first he wasn't overly impressed by this small, dark bird. But then it darted into a patch of sunlight; its feathers flashed like amethysts and emeralds, brilliantly iridescent, fleetingly and gloriously beautiful.

"Pretty, isn't it?" Rowan said casually.

"Exquisite," he said, making no attempt to mask his delight.

Rowan frowned at him. The Brant of old would no more have spent time watching a hummingbird than he would have canceled one of his own trips for her sake. He looked relaxed, she thought. As though he were enjoying himself. And that, too, was new.

Feeling uneasy and on edge, she folded the scope. Five minutes further along the trail she found another Carib, this time perched on a tiny, cup-shaped nest in the shade. "Is it a male or a female?" Natalie asked, focusing her camera.

"Female." Rowan looked right at Brant. "The pair bond lasts two or three seconds and then the male's gone."

Her chin was tilted. *We went to bed together that last night,* she was saying. *But then you left, didn't you? You left me alone for eight months.*

He had. She'd begged him not to go to Colombia that last time and he'd paid her no attention. She was using female intuition, so he'd told her, as a ploy to try and get her own way. Three weeks into his stay he'd been ab-ducted, along with Gabrielle; ironically, both he and Gabrielle had been hired as negotiators to obtain the release of some oil company engineers who'd been kidnapped by the same group of rebels.

His eyes fell from the blatant challenge in Rowan's gaze, his fragile sense of peace shattered. In the four years of their marriage, had he ever changed his plans for her? As he sought through his memories, he could only conclude that he hadn't. His job was much too important for that. He earned five times her salary; his articles helped mold opinion in high places around the globe, and exposed atrocities that dictators the world over didn't want to appear in print. Whereas all she did was find birds.

Birds that had made his soul exult with their beauty.

More confused than he'd ever been in his life, Brant saw Rowan check her watch. They turned back, wending their way to the van and then driving to the hotel. Dinner remained a blur in his mind; he listened as Rowan outlined the plans for tomorrow, and escaped as soon as he could. In his room he thumbed through the bird book for a while and read a couple of chapters in the very badly written espionage novel he'd picked up in Toronto's Terminal Two. Although the room felt too small to contain him, he had no desire to head for the nearest bar. In Grenada all that had gotten him was a hangover the next day.

He'd go for a swim. If he didn't soon burn off some energy, he'd go nuts.

The moon was three-quarters full and the lights from the hotel glimmered on the water. The repetitive slosh of waves on the sand sounded very soothing. He strode past the bar, where Steve was chatting up one of the other female guests and Natalie was sitting with Sheldon and Karen, drinking rum punch and looking thoroughly bored. Quickly he dropped his towel on the sand and ran into the water, heading straight out in a fast crawl.

Away from the lot of them. But mostly away from his own thoughts.

There were powerboats and yachts anchored offshore. Brant swam around them, glad to be out of sight of the hotel; then he set off for the rocky point to the south of the hotel, swimming more easily now, enjoying the splashing in his ears and the pull of his muscles against the water's resistance. The moonlight that dipped and swayed on the swell was a cold, luminous white. Rowan had been cold toward him, cold and distant. Wasn't it up to him to ignite her to the fire and heat of the sun? All alone like this, feeling oddly peaceful, that didn't seem so impossible a task.

He pulled himself up on the rocks and sat for a while, until he started to get cold. Needing to get his blood moving, he set off at a jog back down the beach toward the hotel.

Halfway along the sand, a figure stepped out of the bushes that edged the hotel grounds. A woman. For a wild moment Brant was sure it was Rowan; in crushing disappointment he realized it was Natalie. She flung herself at him, winding her arms around his waist and leaning all her weight on him. He staggered, put his own arms around her to keep his balance and said flatly, "Natalie, I don't need this."

She smelled strongly of rum. She said blearily, "Sure you do...I'll give you a good time, I've wanted to go to bed with you ever since I saw you at breakfast that first day, you're just the kind of guy who turns me on."

She rather spoiled this speech by ending it with a hiccup. Brant set her firmly on her feet and moved back two paces. She was wearing a minidress that left little to the imagination and she was smiling at him, running her tongue over her full lips. "Steve is the one who turns you on," he said, wondering if it was true. "You're only doing this to make him jealous."

She reached out one hand and ran it down his body from breastbone to navel. "Don't make me laugh. You've got a great body."

Her caress left him as cold as the moonlight. "I'm not available."

She sidled closer. "Oh, yes, you are...although you do take the cake for being uptight. Wound up tighter than a drum, what's your problem?"

He wouldn't have expected her to be so perceptive. "If I've got a problem," he said wryly, "it's not your job to solve it. Make up with Steve...that's what you really want to do."

Her lip quivered. She sagged against him, wailing, "I asked him to marry me a week ago and he says he's not ready to settle down, and look at him at the bar sucking up to that blonde, I hate him, I hate his guts..."

She was sobbing now, luxuriantly prolonged sobs that Brant was sure everyone at the hotel could hear. "Natalie," he said with all the force of his personality, "shove it! It's the rum that's crying, not you, and maybe you should sit down somewhere all by yourself and think about what you really want out of life." Advice it wouldn't hurt him to take himself, he thought ruefully.

"I want y-you," she snuffled.

"I'm not your type any more than you're mine."

Her head reared up. "Right," she said venomously, "I've watched you, you've only got eyes for Rowan. Well, you can have her, the stuck-up bitch—I'm going back to the bar."

She set off unsteadily across the sand. Brant ran his fingers through his wet hair. He'd tried.

Much good had it done him.

He'd give her five minutes and then he'd get his towel and go to bed. Did every other member of the group think he only had eyes for Rowan?

Peg and May sure did.

Hell, thought Brant. Hell and damnation.

A voice wafted across the water, a voice full of mockery. "You missed your chance there, Brant."

The hair rose on the back of his neck. He looked out to sea, and saw a dark head, dark as a seal's, swimming toward the shore. Rowan.

Great. So she'd been a witness to that little fiasco. He said nastily, "This whole trip is rapidly turning into farce— remember that play we saw in London, the one where people kept bursting through all those doors? All we need now is Steve to blunder his way down the beach."

"Oh, no," Rowan said, "you've got it wrong. All we need now is Gabrielle."

She was standing up in thigh-deep water, moonlight glinting on her wet skin and on a one-piece swimsuit that clung to her body. His heart was jouncing in his chest as though he were seventeen, not thirty-seven. Bluntly he stated the obvious. "I sure don't need Gabrielle here."

The air was cool on Rowan's skin; but she scarcely noticed. In an effort to settle her jangled nerves before bed, she'd swum out behind the nearest moored powerboats, and it was from there that she'd heard Natalie's proposition, and her subsequent sobs and wails. Infuriated that everyone in the group now seemed to be aware of the tension between her and Brant, she'd then made the mistake of alerting Brant to her presence.

So much for keeping her cool.

Distantly aware that the water was to her knees now, wavelets rippling on the shore, Rowan said with icy clarity, "Oh? So you've dumped Gabrielle, too? She only lasted three years to my four? Dear me."

Brant's jaw tightened, his throat muscles corded like rope. "How about a little reality check here? You can't dump someone you've never had."

"Oh, for God's sake!" Rowan exploded. "Why don't

you give up this fiction that you and Gabrielle weren't lovers? I *hate* it when you lie to me.''

"I've never lied to you about Gabrielle!''

All the pain and rage of the last two years seized Rowan in their fangs. "I saw you, Brant,'' she seethed. "The day I went to the hospital, the same day I got back from Greenland.''

"I don't have a clue what you're talking about.''

"I stood in the doorway of your room and watched you for a full five seconds that felt as long as a lifetime. You had your arms around each other, you and Gabrielle, and your cheek was resting on her hair. You were whispering something to her, heaven knows what…but do you know what was the worst? The expression on your face.'' In spite of herself, Rowan heard her voice break. "You looked so—so tender. So loving. I thought I was the only woman who called that up in you. I was your wife, after all. But that was the day I realized I'd been supplanted.'' She scrubbed at her cheeks, where tears were mingling with drops of salt water. "So I left. And I never came back.''

Feeling as though someone had hit him with a two-by-four, Brant said helplessly, "My God, Rowan…'' and all the while he was searching his memory for the details of the scene that must have, he realized with a sick lurch of his gut, cost him his marriage. "I didn't even see you…''

"Of course you didn't, you only had eyes for her. That's the whole point,'' Rowan said bitterly.

By now she was standing a couple of feet away from him. She was crying. But some deep intuition warned Brant against reaching out for her, even though he craved to do so. "For the last two years I've thought you didn't care enough about me to come to the hospital,'' he said. "That you'd condemned me for infidelity without even giving me a chance to defend myself.''

"Oh, I cared. More fool me."

"I remember that day now," he said slowly. "Gabrielle was on the same floor as me, she'd had dengue fever, as well. And they kept trying to foist psychiatrists on both of us, I remember that, too. She'd—"

"Brant, I don't even want to talk about it," Rowan snapped. "I know what I saw. No explanation that you can conjure up two years later is going to convince me otherwise."

He fought down an anger that if he gave it rein would ruin everything. "Tell me something," he said levelly. "Up until I went away that last time, had I ever lied to you?"

"No," she said unwillingly. "I know there was stuff you didn't tell me about your trips, even though I begged you to. A whole lot of stuff. To protect me. Or yourself. But I don't think you ever lied." Again she swiped at her wet cheeks. "Why should you? You hadn't met Gabrielle."

Brant said forcefully, "In the three years I've known Gabrielle, I've never once made love to her. Or wanted to."

Rowan flinched. "Don't! Don't do this to me, Brant. You wouldn't be the first man to be unfaithful to his wife and I'm sure you won't be the last. Just don't lie about it."

There was a band around his chest squeezing the air from his lungs and he had no idea what to say next. "Dammit, I'm not lying!"

"Let me tell you something else. I was in Greenland sledding across the sea ice when you were released. So I didn't know anything about it until I landed in Resolute Bay. There were newspapers there, full of how you and Gabrielle had been imprisoned together. Full of innuendos. The photos showed the two of you holding on to each other at the Miami airport, then arriving in Toronto together— you were holding her hand by the ambulance." She dragged air into her throat. "I saw all that. And, of course, I'd lived through eight months of knowing you and she were together. But I still trusted you. So as soon as I got back to Toronto, I went to the hospital to see you."

She ran her fingers through her cropped curls. "I saw you, all right. That's when I realized you loved her, not me. That I'd been a fool to trust you." She gulped in more air. "What would you have believed, Brant? If it had been you standing in the doorway of that hospital room, watching me and another man in each other's arms? A man I'd spent the last eight months with."

His tongue felt thick in his mouth. "I'd probably have believed the worst. Like you did."

Her shoulders sagged; somehow she'd needed to hear him say that. "Well. You know the rest. I got a lawyer and a year later we were divorced." It hadn't been quite as simple as that. There was one particular secret from the last three years that she'd never shared with anyone, a secret laced with pain and guilt; nor was she about to share it now. Not with Brant.

Natalie's loud sobs had left Brant unmoved. Rowan's silent weeping rended his heart. He said quietly, risking a step closer to her so he could wipe her wet cheek, "Rowan, you're cold and it's late. But I really need you to hear me out. To try and listen with an open mind."

"My towel's around here somewhere," she said vaguely.

He looked around, saw the dark shape lying on the sand a few feet away and picked it up. Taking another risk, he draped it over her shoulders and watched her tug it around her body. In a small voice she said, "Okay—I'll listen."

He'd been afraid she'd say no. His own throat was clogged with emotion. But of course he never cried; hadn't shed a tear since the year his mother had died when he'd been five and his father had come home to take over his upbringing. Which was, he thought grimly, nothing whatsoever to do with Rowan.

He cudgeled his brain, desperate to convince her of the truth. "Three things," he said. "First of all, that day in the hospital was the day Gabrielle broke. She'd been incredibly brave through the whole eight months, but that morning her doctor had ordered some resident in psychiatry to see her, a young pup who insisted she had to process and integrate, you know the kind of jargon they use. She fled to my room and started to cry...she's like you, she hardly ever cries. And yes, I was holding her, and yes, there'd have been tenderness, even love, in my face because she and I had been through a lot together..."

Rowan stood very still. She was shivering, although not altogether from cold, the scene in the hospital room etched as clearly in her mind as if it were yesterday. "Go on," she muttered.

He'd sworn he'd never tell anyone what he was about to tell Rowan. But if ever there was a time to break one of his own rules, this was it. "The second thing is this, and don't ask me to explain it because I can't. Somehow Gabrielle in that eight months became the mother I missed so badly when I was a little boy...the sister I never had. I couldn't have gone to bed with her. It would have been like incest. If I love Gabrielle, Rowan, I love her like a sister." His laugh was humorless. "That sounds so damned corny."

It did. It also sounded peculiarly convincing. Rowan buried her chin in her towel. "Number three?" she said neutrally.

"That's easy. I wouldn't be standing here if it wasn't for Gabrielle. You see, her best friend Sonia Williams is the wife of Rick Williams, the fellow with pneumonia." Quickly he described the scene in Gabrielle's apartment last

Sunday, marveling that it was less than a week ago when it felt like a lifetime. "Gabrielle's the one who told me—in no uncertain terms—that I needed to see you."

She also thinks I still love you. But that was number four and he'd only promised three. He clamped his mouth shut, waiting for Rowan's response.

For what seemed like forever she was silent, the waves splashing gently on the shore, the moon rocking on the water behind her. Brant said in a cracked voice, "Don't you believe a word I've said?"

Finally Rowan looked up. It was odd, she thought, that after everything he'd told her, all she could feel was a dull ache somewhere in the vicinity of her heart. "I don't know what to think," she mumbled. "I—I guess I believe you."

She didn't sound convinced and she looked unutterably sad. Brant wanted more from her than that halfhearted avowal, a great deal more. Trying to smother his disappointment, searching for a kind of wisdom and restraint he'd never felt the need for before, he said with a twisted smile, "I think it's past time you went to bed, Rowan. Sleep on it, and we'll talk again tomorrow."

She nodded like a marionette on a string. "Okay," she said again.

Brant put an arm lightly around her shoulders and steered her toward the path to the hotel, remembering to pick up his own towel on the way. Five people were left in the bar, one of them Steve, now minus both Natalie and the blonde. Steve got to his feet, staggered over to them and said truculently, "He bothering you, Rowan?"

"No," Rowan said coldly.

"You sure?"

"Back off," Brant said in a tone of voice he used rarely but always to good effect.

Steve blinked. "If she wants to be left alone, then that's

what you oughta do," he pronounced with an air of profundity.

Brant might have laughed had Steve's words not been so unpleasantly near the truth. "I'll remember that," he said, and continued along the concrete pathway between the mounds of bougainvillea. When he came to the door of Rowan's room, he kissed her lips, which were cold, and said, "Thanks for listening."

His big body was so close Rowan could have tangled her fingers in the dark pelt on his chest. She'd never forgotten a single detail of Brant's body, not how he looked or felt, nor how he used to move against her own body with a sensuality she'd adored. Even the scent of his skin, salty now from the sea, was utterly familiar to her.

A great wave of terror washed over her. Clumsily she tugged the room key from around her neck and unlocked the door. "Good night," she said, scurried through the opening and shut the door in his face. Her knees were trembling and every muscle she owned ached. She stumbled to the bathroom, put the plug in the tub and turned on the hot tap.

CHAPTER FIVE

ROWAN was dreaming.

She was playing basketball, an all-important champion-ship game that would determine whether her team got into the finals. The crowd was screaming in the background. Then she saw that the member of the opposing team whom she'd been assigned to guard was Brant: angry, sweaty, and altogether too large. She dodged, she ducked, she darted back and forth on the floor, her legs aching, her stomach tied in knots, and knew in her heart it was hopeless. She couldn't possibly outwit him.

A piercing beep signaled time-out.

Rowan found herself sitting bolt upright in bed, and jammed down the button on her alarm clock to stop its insistent summons. Her ears were ringing with the feral roar of the crowd and her belly was clenched with remembered fear.

Except it wasn't fear that was clenching her belly. It was a cramp. Oh, no, she groaned inwardly, leaning forward to ease the pain. Not today.

Rapidly she ran her mind back over the calendar. She was two days early. Stress, so they said, could do that to you.

Today they had the longest hike of the whole trip, and she had a picnic lunch to organize. She had to keep Steve and Natalie from each other's throats, she had to find a perched parrot for May and Peg, and she had to deal with Brant.

Just a regular day, she thought wryly. Right off the bat

she'd take one of the pills her doctor had prescribed for the first day of her period. She didn't like taking pills. But this was one time her principles could fly out the window.

Brant. He'd been telling the truth about Gabrielle last night on the beach, she was almost sure of it. So where did that leave her? Aside from late for breakfast.

Totally confused, that's where.

Rowan scrambled out of bed, showered in the hottest water she could bear, letting it beat on her lower back, and got dressed, picking out her favorite tangerine shirt. The hot water had given her face a tinge of color; she brushed her hair, put on some lipstick and gave herself an encouraging grin in the steamy mirror. She'd go out there and she'd do her job. No arguments with Brant, and if Steve and Natalie stepped out of line, she'd cream them. Diplomatically, of course.

She laced up her boots and left the room, and it seemed a good omen that in the dining room Peg was seated on one side of Brant and May on the other, and that all three were embroiled in a discussion about agronomics.

What Rowan knew about agronomics could have been put on the blade of a hoe. She smiled brightly at Steve, who looked rather the worse for wear, and started asking him about the scuba diving business he owned in Boston.

So what if she'd had a ridiculous dream about basketball? Everything was going to be fine today.

Rowan's optimism lasted through breakfast and most of the drive to the rain forest. But as the van jounced and bounced over the potholes in the road, the effects of the pill she'd taken began to wear off. While it wasn't an overly strenuous hike to the parrot look-off, it was considerably further than they'd gone yesterday; and there were lots of stops along the way, all of which involved either standing as she searched the dense greenery with her binoculars, or else bending over the scope. Her backache got worse; she tried her best to breathe her way through the cramps without being too obvious about it.

When they finally reached the look-off, the whole group got to see the graceful soaring of a black hawk over the canopy of trees; this island was their only chance to see the hawk's elegant black and white plumage and hooked yellow bill, so Rowan was delighted that it had appeared so readily.

Brant saw her pleasure. He also noticed, because he knew her well, that some kind of strain underlay this pleasure and that she was avoiding eye contact with him.

Several parrots—always in pairs, Brant couldn't help noticing—flapped across the gap in the trees, the gold on their wings in striking contrast to the green slopes of the mountains, their raucous calls echoing in the deep valley. They left Brant feeling edgy and uncertain; nor had the rain forest brought him the transitory peace of yesterday.

Rowan looked terrible.

She might be deceiving the others; but because all his senses were attuned to her, he was acutely aware of the pallor in her cheeks and the shadows under her eyes. She didn't look like a woman who'd discovered the night before that her ex-husband hadn't been unfaithful to her. Or else the discovery had brought her no joy.

She looked so weighed down and exhausted that he longed to comfort her. He could cheerfully have throttled sweet-natured Karen who wanted help in seeing vireos, hummingbirds, and then the two parrots that were obliging enough to perch in a tree on the far side of the valley.

There was no faulting Rowan's patience, nor her genuine pleasure when Karen suddenly gasped, "Oh, *that* tree! Now I see them—oh, aren't they beautiful!"

The rest of the group was focusing on the parrots. Brant

watched Rowan lean back against one of the vertical posts that supported the roof of the look-off, and shut her eyes. The slender line of her legs in their bush pants, the curve of her hips and jut of her breasts all filled him with a frantic longing. But overriding his rampant sexual needs was something new. The desire to protect her. To cherish her and look after her.

Was this really a new feeling? Surely not. He and Rowan had lived as husband and wife for four years, it couldn't be new. He'd been a good husband...hadn't he?

His hiking boots soundless on the grass, Brant stepped closer. "Rowan..." he said softly.

Her eyes flew open to meet his, and she pushed away from the post. She didn't say a word. She didn't need to. He got the message anyway.

Get lost. Now.

Then her face constricted with pain and, as if she couldn't help herself, she hunched forward over her belly.

Brant, you idiot, he thought in a great surge of relief. This is physiological, not emotional. First day of the month. Rowan always had cramps that day. He said in a fierce whisper, "I'm carrying the scope on the way back, as well as that bloody great camera in your haversack, and don't you dare argue."

Slowly she straightened, trying to breathe deep to relieve the pain. "I sure wish you'd mind your own business."

"I can't," he said with raw truth.

"Then try harder."

"Rowan, I—"

Through gritted teeth she said, "Brant, go take a hike."

Sheldon called, "The first one's just flown. There goes the other one—can you find them in the scope again, Rowan?"

"I'll give it a try," she said with a cheerfulness that irked the hell out of Brant. But that was her job, of course. To find birds and be nice to her clients.

She wasn't wasting many of her niceties on him.

He undid her haversack for the second time and put her camera in his own bag. When they were leaving the look-off half an hour later, he pushed past Steve and put his hand on the tripod just as Rowan did. "I'll carry it," he said loud enough for everyone to hear, and felt her fingers dig into his in impotent fury.

He grinned at her, daring her to make an issue of it. "Don't worry, I'll stick close to you," he added, "so you can use it whenever you need to."

"Thank you, Brant," Rowan said in a honeyed voice, "you're so thoughtful."

You're an arrogant bastard, was what she really meant. "You're welcome," he said with his very best smile.

He kept to her heels all the way back to the picnic site, ignoring the waves of antagonism coming from both Steve and Natalie. Not to mention Rowan. It started to rain, drops pattering on the leaves; when they emerged at the picnic site, the mountain crests were hidden in thick gray cloud and the grass was drenched.

Bent over under the small corrugated tin overhang of the park headquarters, which was tightly locked, Rowan mixed tortellini with artichoke halves, sun-dried tomatoes, Parmesan and an olive oil dressing, and cut up green onions and cucumber for the tabbouleh. The others were huddled against the wall. Her back was killing her.

The sun came out again as they were finishing eating. Rowan cleaned up the leftovers and reloaded the van, and they drove to the Botanic Gardens in Kingstown, making a couple of stops on the way for shorebirds. While the cramps didn't seem to be abating very much, she was reluctant to take a second pill because they made her drowsy and heavy-headed.

There was a captive breeding program for the parrots at the gardens; as the rest of the group milled around the big cages and took pictures of the birds and of the dramatic scarlet and yellow heliconia flowers, Brant saw that Rowan was standing by herself, staring into the farthest cage. He stationed himself beside her, watching the parrots cling to the metal wire. "Neither of us ever liked zoos," he ventured.

"No," she said, her gaze fixed on the birds. "I just have to hope this is doing some good, increasing their population so they won't get extinct."

He didn't want to talk about the population dynamics of parrots. "I'm sorry you're feeling lousy. That first day always was bad for you, wasn't it?"

She turned to face him, her brown eyes openly unfriendly. "I'm not asking you for sympathy. I'm not asking you for anything."

His lashes flickered. "So you didn't believe me last night."

"Yes, I did. But it doesn't make any difference, don't you see?"

"Can't say that I do," he retorted.

Her brow crinkled. "Well, actually that's not strictly true, it did sort of make a difference. I feel better knowing you didn't lie to me, that you weren't unfaithful with Gabrielle. It's very strange." Absorbedly, she ran her fingers down the small metal squares of the cage. "I haven't given it a lot of thought because I've been feeling so awful all day. But I'd have to say I feel looser. Freer. As though I can let you go more easily now, because I know you didn't cheat on me with another woman."

Brant suddenly felt like the one in the cage, a cage that

was shrinking fast, pressing in on him on every side. He said hoarsely, "Freer? *That's* how you feel?"

"I know it's not logical," she answered with a helpless shrug.

"Is that what you want?" he rapped, hearing each word fall like a stone from his lips. "To be free of me?"

She glanced around. The others had headed toward a jacaranda tree whose blooms were a mist of purple, and would be, she knew from past experience, alive with hummingbirds. She should be there with them; but they could wait for a few minutes. With passionate intensity she said, "Brant, I've been like a robot the last couple of years. Separated but not separated, free to date but not wanting to, alone in my bed and with no desire to put anyone else there in your place. I'm thirty-one years old. I've got to move on—and the sooner the better. We've both got to. I'm beginning to think Gabrielle was right, you did need to see me. Just as I needed to see you." She managed a smile. "Smart woman, that."

Brant was sweating in the ninety-degree heat, yet his hands felt like chunks of ice. He was the one who'd sworn to Gabrielle that he was through with Rowan. That they were divorced in all senses of the word. He was also the one who supposedly didn't tell lies.

So where did that leave him?

In bad trouble, that's where.

"Rowan," he stumbled, "Gabrielle being like a sister to me wasn't the only reason I didn't sleep with—"

"Sorry, I've got to go, Natalie's waving."

His feet felt like chunks of ice, too. Weighted to the spot, Brant watched her hurry around the corner of the cage toward the jacaranda tree. He hadn't slept with Gabrielle because he loved Rowan. Loved her? Past tense? Or, despite all his protestations to the contrary, did he still love her?

She wanted to move on. To another man and another life, one that didn't include him.

He'd kill the son of a bitch and ask questions afterward.

Sure, Brant, he jeered. You know damn well you won't do that. Because if Rowan really wants to be free, there's not one solitary thing in the whole wide world you can do to stop her. Not one. You'd have to let her go.

He realized he was gripping the cage so tightly that his knuckles were white as bone. Rage, sexual frustration, and a sense of utter powerlessness were part of that grip; and all these emotions were fueled by a stark and unrelenting fear.

A lot of his assignments had made him feel afraid, although never to this crippling level. But powerlessness was a new sensation. He wasn't used to that.

He rubbed his hands down the sides of his jeans. He had to pull himself together; the others would be wondering what the devil was wrong with him, cowering behind a cageful of parrots. Basically he didn't care if he ever saw another parrot. He had more important things on his mind. Like what his next strategy should be.

He'd told Rowan the truth about Gabrielle. She'd believed him. But all he'd accomplished was to drive her further away. It was going to be hard to top that for sheer incompetence, he thought acerbically. Come on, buddy, you're supposed to be the guy with brains, the expert at getting out of tight corners. Or so your boss thinks. So why don't you put some of your expertise to use as far as your ex-wife's concerned?

He trailed across the gardens between royal palms and cannonball trees, between billows of bougainvillea and the scarlet spikes of heliconia. Steve was carrying the scope, but not even this could shift Brant's brain into any gear other than reverse.

He quite literally didn't know what to do next. Was this why he was so frightened? Or was it the prospect of Rowan in another man's arms that was making his armpits run with sweat and his blood thrum in his ears?

He followed the rest of them back to the van; he had a shower in his room, then trailed to the dining room for dinner. Rowan had put on makeup along with a bright orange silk shirt; with a nasty tightening of his nerves he saw she was wearing earrings, ceramic earrings shaped like rowanberries that matched her shirt. Brant ordered smoked fish and tried to quell the anger roiling in his gut. How was he to interpret her gesture except as a supreme indifference toward him and his long-ago gift? Toward the love that had been behind that gift?

To hell with fancy strategies. He was going to find out if she was indifferent to him and he was going to do it soon. And he wasn't going to be fussy about his methods.

He didn't bother ordering coffee, left the table before her, and strode down the corridor toward her room, which was in the other wing from his. Tucking himself into an alcove along with a potted, spiky and extremely ugly cactus, he waited for her to arrive. He didn't know what he was going to say. But he sure knew what he was going to do.

It was ten years since he'd had a cigarette and he'd give his eyeteeth for one right now. Brant jammed his hands in his pockets and waited. Five minutes passed, another five, and then he heard the soft pad of steps along the brick walk that connected the rooms. The steps stopped at Rowan's door. Moving with calculated slowness, he risked peering around the edge of the alcove.

Rowan's back was half turned to him. She was searching her pockets for her key, finally locating it in her hip pocket. Then she dropped it. She said a very pithy word that brought an involuntary grin to his lips, and stooped to pick it up. Then she wearily rubbed the small of her back. If she'd been pale earlier, she looked like a ghost in the dusk.

She also looked like a woman at the end of her tether. Brant's heart constricted with compassion. He couldn't confront her now. No matter how angry and afraid he was.

As he eased back into the alcove, a cactus spike stabbed the back of his knee; although he managed to smother his instinctive yelp of pain, the heel of his hiking boot struck the side of the pot. Rowan called out sharply, "Who's there?"

Feeling utterly foolish, Brant stepped out into the open. "It's me. But I wasn't going to—"

"I should have known it would be you!"

"I'd changed my mind, I wasn't—"

She rolled right over him. "You never give up, do you? I suppose that's why you're such a good journalist—but it sure doesn't impress me right now."

"Oh, quit it, Rowan! You don't need to be so goddamned argumentative. What you need to do is stop talking, spend an hour in a Jacuzzi and then get three nights' sleep."

She thrust the key into the lock. "I know I look awful, I don't need you telling me."

He said rashly, "When we were married, this was the night I used to rub your back."

"On the rare occasions when you were home," she flashed. "Which was probably one month out of six."

Stung, Brant said, "I had a job to do."

"Yes, you did. Job first, Rowan second. Too bad you didn't explain that to me before we got married."

"You wouldn't have listened," he snarled. "You wanted to marry me just as much as I wanted to marry you."

"So here's another cliché you can add to your collection—marry in haste, repent at leisure."

In the dim light her eyes were like pools of lava. Brant seized her by the elbows, yanked her against the length of his body and kissed her hard on the mouth. That, at least, had been part of his strategy.

Her body was as rigid as a board and between one moment and the next all his anger collapsed. Rowan was in his arms again after an absence that felt like forever. The blood beating in his ears, Brant slid his hands up her arms to her shoulders, kneading them gently with his fingers, and softened his kiss, seeking to evoke the response that had always been there for him. With his tongue he stroked the soft curve of her lip. One hand drifted down her back to gather her closer, soothing the knotted muscles of her spine.

For Rowan it was as though time had gone backward. She could have been in their condo in Toronto, and Brant come home to her after one of his trips: the hard curve of his rib cage, the taut throat, the scent and heat of his skin all achingly familiar and horribly missed. She wound her arms around his neck, digging her nails into the thickness of his hair, and opened to the thrust of his tongue. Heaven, she thought dazedly. Sheer heaven.

Brant felt her surrender surge through his body. Exultant, he found the rise of her breast beneath the orange silk of her shirt, cupping its softness, fiercely hungry to taste the ivory of her skin and the dusky, hard-tipped nipple. She gasped with pleasure, her body arching to his touch in the way that had always made him feel both conqueror and conquered. Then her hand fumbled for the buttons on his shirt, thrusting itself against his belly.

Leaving a trail of kisses down her throat, Brant muttered, "It's been so long...too long."

Rowan's fingertips teased the tangle of his body hair and laved the tautness of muscle. She didn't want to talk. She didn't want to think. All she wanted to do was feel. Touch.

Caress. Stroke. Luxuriate in everything she'd been deprived of. She rubbed her hips against his, and in an explosion of hunger as scarlet as a hibiscus blossom felt the hardness of Brant's erection.

His kiss deepened. Rhythmically his thumb abraded her breast, back and forth, back and forth, until she was drowning in a sea of scarlet petals.

Then, like a knife clipping a blossom from the stem, a small voice pierced the red haze of desire that had enveloped her. *You mustn't make love with Brant. He's not your husband anymore. You're divorced. Remember?*

In a crazy counterpoint to her thoughts she heard him say, "Let me spend the night with you, sweetheart...I want to hold you in my arms and never let you go."

It was as though ice-cold water had been dashed in Rowan's face: pleasure vanished and hunger was eclipsed by a panic as elemental as a hurricane. She shoved against Brant's chest with all her strength. "Don't call me sweetheart, I'm not your sweetheart anymore," she cried; then watched as, with enormous effort, he brought himself back to the harsh reality of her words.

He said forcibly, "I don't tell lies."

"Neither do I!"

"Rowan, don't try and tell me we're through with each other. That kiss proves otherwise."

She said in a clipped voice, "I haven't been to bed with anyone since the night you left for Colombia. Which, as you may recall, was nearly three years ago. Of course I'm going to fall all over you, I'm only human and we always liked sex."

"*Liked* it? It was a lot more than liking."

"So what? You're not spending the night with me. Not now or ever again."

"You make it sound as though there was nothing between us but sex!"

"There were times when I wondered," she said with the same glacial precision.

He whispered, "You can't mean that."

Did she mean it, Rowan wondered, or was she guilty of distorting the truth just so he'd leave her alone? So she wouldn't have to remember the woman who a few moments ago had rediscovered the heaven that lay in Brant's arms? "I mean it," she said in a low voice, knowing if she didn't get rid of him soon she'd lose it, pour out all the frustrations and deprivations of her marriage to the man who'd been their cause yet who'd remained oblivious to them.

"For God's sake," Brant muttered, "how can you say something so untrue?"

He looked stricken. She wanted to weep, she wanted to scream out her rage at the top of her lungs; she did neither one. She did know she'd had enough. More than enough. "I told you in Grenada to fly right back to Toronto," she said tightly. "I don't want you here stirring up the past, Brant. It's an exercise in futility."

Like a robot repeating a learned phrase, he said, "Of course—you want to move on." Then all his bitterness spilled out. "To a better man than me."

His words were like a trigger; Rowan abandoned all her good intentions. "That's right," she seethed. "To a man who's there at night when my cramps are so bad I need a backrub to go to sleep. Someone I can depend on to be around when we've made vacation plans—"

"It was only once—that time I had to go to Pakistan—that we had to cancel our plans."

Furiously she ticked off her fingers. "What about the trip we planned to Fiji? And to Antarctica? Were you available? No, you'd gone to South Africa the first time and to

Indonesia the second, because your precious boss had phoned. Drop everything, scrap a silly little vacation with your wife, you've got more important things to do." To her fury her voice cracked. "I want stability, Brant. I want someone safe, so I don't have to lie awake at nights worrying where you are and whose feathers you're ruffling and whether you've stepped on a land mine or got in the way of a submachine gun—and I don't think that's much to ask."

"I always came back to you!"

"You spent eight months in the company of another woman and I don't give a sweet damn how platonic it was!"

"Maybe you've forgotten it was my job that paid for the fancy condo on the shores of the lake—we sure couldn't have afforded it on your salary."

Rowan's breath hissed between her teeth. "I've always known you looked down on my job, you never made any secret of that. And let me tell you something else—I live in the country now. In a cabin that's only big enough for me. And I like it just fine."

Knowing he was behaving execrably, Brant grated, "Then go find yourself a farmer whose biggest excitement of the week is spreading cow manure on the back pasture."

"Don't tempt me." Her eyes narrowed. "But first, why don't you tell me something, Brant? Where have your assignments taken you the last couple of years?"

He didn't even have to think. "Sudan, Turkey, Cambodia, Peru. Why?"

As Rowan's temper fizzled out like a spent firecracker, tiredness settled on her shoulders. What had she hoped for? That he might say England? Switzerland? The Bahamas? Safe, ordinary places? This was Brant, for goodness' sake. "You've got to have danger, haven't you?" she said.

"You've got to have your fix. That's what really destroyed our marriage, Brant. Because it truly is over. Finished. I won't go through another eight months like that ever again. Not for any man."

She could hear the finality in her voice. Brant went very still, a stillness like paralysis, and suddenly Rowan knew she couldn't bear prolonging this confrontation any longer. She reached up on tiptoes, kissed him lightly on the lips and whispered, "Good night, Brant. And goodbye." Then she turned away so he couldn't see her face.

Her key turned smoothly in the lock and the door swung open. Rowan hurried into her room, closed the door behind her and snagged the lock on the inside, sliding the chain into its metal groove.

Not that there was any real need to rush. Or to lock the door so securely. Brant was still standing on the brick walkway, his eyes stunned, his face a mask of disbelief and pain. It was the wrong moment to be torn by an intuition that she was betraying something infinitely precious. That she should stay and fight for it, not run away.

She was tired of fighting. She'd done too much of it over the four years of their marriage.

Not even bothering to take off her clothes, Rowan threw herself across the bed and started to cry, bunching her pillow over her head so Brant wouldn't hear her. And if she'd been asked she couldn't have said whether she was crying for Brant, for herself, or for the frailty of all that had bound them together.

Or for the utter finality of that one small word, goodbye.

CHAPTER SIX

OUTSIDE, Brant tried to pull himself together. Another cliché, he thought distantly. But true. All too true. The reason he had to pull himself together was because he felt like he was falling apart. Walking slowly, like a much older man, he headed for the bar, taking the table that was nearest to the beach and the ripple of the sea.

The rum punch he ordered was altogether too sweet, while the fruit floating in it turned his stomach. For the better part of an hour he stared out at the yachts anchored offshore, something in his demeanor keeping the other vacationers and the waiter a safe distance away. What had Gabrielle said? All your feelings are buried, gone underground; or something to that effect. She should see him now. He was nothing but feeling, a mass of raw and extraordinarily unpleasant feeling.

Maybe this was why people kept their emotions buried. It would make sense, wouldn't it? Why would anyone want to submit themselves to this kind of pain if they had a choice?

The moon glistened on the sea. A perfect recipe for romance, he thought, especially when you added palm trees, hibiscus and pale sand. All he needed was a woman. But for him there was only one woman who could bring all those other ingredients to life. A red-haired woman with a turbulent temper and a body that ignited his own. Rowan.

He'd been royally kidding himself for the last two years; he was no more through with her than he was with breathing.

79

But she was through with him. She'd made that all too clear this evening. The marriage is over, she'd said. Finished. According to her, he'd destroyed it: partly by his unspoken but very real belittlement of her job; but much more so by his need to live with danger, to push to the limits his courage and his powers of endurance. Regardless of the cost to her.

He couldn't bear it.

The ice had melted in his rum punch. He left it sitting on the table and walked away from the bar, stumbling along the beach to the rocks where he'd swum last night. It felt like a lifetime ago. It was a lifetime ago. Because last night he'd still had the hope that somehow he'd win Rowan back. And now he had none.

Sitting down on a boulder, Brant buried his head in his hands.

Rowan managed to wake five minutes before the alarm the next morning. The cramps were gone until next month, she knew that from experience. If only Brant would disappear as easily.

Brant, and all her tangled feelings for him.

She got out of bed and went to the bathroom, where she started to brush her teeth. She looked exactly like a woman who'd cried herself to sleep and who'd had the worst fight of her whole life with a man who had only to kiss her and she'd melt in his arms.

Sex. she thought fiercely. It was only sex.

Still, she looked a great deal better right now than Brant had looked last night. Staring at the white foam on the brush as though she'd never seen toothpaste before, Rowan felt her belly contract. She'd never seen him look so desolate. So heartsick.

All his emotions right there on the surface.

She gaped at herself in the mirror. That was it. That was what was new. Brant, as well she knew, was a man who only showed his feelings when he was in bed with her: that had always been the pattern of their marriage. She'd been content with that pattern until the last year they'd lived together, when things had really begun to fall apart. Two months before he'd left on that last assignment, she'd accused him of being the inventor of male detachment and the stiff upper lip, and he hadn't bothered denying it. So what had changed him?

Not your concern, Rowan. Not anymore. You severed any lingering connections between you and Brant last night when you told him the marriage was over.

Tears brimmed in her eyes and overflowed down her cheeks, dripping into the sink along with the toothpaste. Oh, damn, she thought helplessly, oh, damn...

With vicious energy she finished cleaning her teeth and splashed her face with cold water. She was going to keep so busy today she wouldn't have the time to think about him. And if that was a form of avoidance, too bad.

She didn't know what else to do.

By ten that morning Rowan had gathered the luggage, checked out of the hotel, reconfirmed the next leg of their journey, exchanged American money for Caribbean dollars and paid the airport taxes, gotten all the boarding passes, and herded the group onto the plane to St. Lucia. Brant, she noticed, spent an inordinate amount of time on the phone at the airport. He was probably talking to his boss, she thought shrewishly, setting up his next trip into danger.

Well, it wouldn't be her worry.

The plane was a Twin Otter and they were jammed in like sardines. In St. Lucia when they went through customs, she discovered the bulk of their luggage had been left behind in St. Vincent. She got everyone to fill in the appropriate forms, then picked up the driver of their van and drove to the hotel.

"Some off time," she said pleasantly to the group. "Lunch at one, and we'll head out to a scrub forest afterward, with the opportunity to see another captive breeding program, this time for the St. Lucia parrots. In the meantime, have a swim in the pool, or snorkel at the beach— it's a five-minute walk from the hotel—and there are some craft shops down the road…enjoy."

"Can I speak to you for a moment, Rowan?" Brant said brusquely.

"Of course," she said with rather overdone politeness, and smiled at the rest of them as they dispersed to their rooms. Bracing herself, she turned to face him.

"When we leave here the day after tomorrow, I won't be going with you to Martinique. I got a flight home via Antigua that day."

His businesslike speech entered Rowan's body like the stab of a dagger. Why hadn't she anticipated this? And wasn't he, after all, merely taking her advice that first night in Grenada? Struggling for composure, she said weakly, "I see."

"I'm going to stay around the hotel this afternoon, too."

"Fine," she said with a mechanical smile.

He nodded, picked up his bag and headed down the path that led to his room; he'd been allotted one with a deck that was laced with vines and further shaded by a deliciously scented frangipani tree. She watched him go, the familiar rangy stride and wide shoulders of the only man she'd ever fallen in love with, and felt a glacial coldness settle on her heart.

This really was the end. When he got on the plane two days from now, she'd never see him again. He'd make sure of that.

She was getting what she wanted and she felt like she was being slowly and agonizingly torn apart.

When Brant went to the bar before dinner, he found Peg and May there before him. "A male Adelaide's warbler," May announced, raising her tankard of local beer.

"And a Lesser Antillean saltator," Peg added, flourishing the little paper umbrella with which her rum punch had been decorated.

"Great," said Brant, who'd hoped for privacy.

"We missed you this afternoon," Peg said.

"You don't look too chipper," May observed. "I hope you're not catching anything, you can't be too careful in the tropics, you know."

Brant, an expert on the tropics, said, "I'm fine."

"Rowan doesn't look her best, either," Peg added.

It was three-quarters of an hour until dinner, there was no one else in the vicinity, and Brant liked both women very much. He said flatly, "I'm Rowan's ex-husband."

Although Peg sucked in her breath, May said, "I'd wondered."

"You had?" Peg said. "You didn't say anything."

"It would have been pure conjecture."

"Gossip," said Peg.

"A pernicious habit," May said loftily. "So why did you come on this trip, Brant?"

She was as bright-eyed as any bird. He said gloomily, "Because I didn't stop to think. Because I'm a prize jerk. Will that do for starters?"

"Were you hoping for a reconciliation?" Peg asked.

"If so, I was what you might call deluded."

"She doesn't want you back?" May asked delicately, sipping her beer.

"She wants me on the first plane back to Toronto. Which I'm taking the day after tomorrow."

"You're leaving us?" Peg said, shocked. "But you won't see the Martinique oriole."

"He won't get back together with Rowan, either," May said sternly. "Is there anything we can do to help?"

Her eyes were kind and he was quite sure she could be discreet. Although he was, from long habit, careful to protect his double identity, he found himself pouring out the story of his marriage, describing his job, their fights, the abduction and Gabrielle, and Rowan's putative visit to the hospital. "I must be a jerk," he finished, waving to the bartender for a refill. "I figured once she knew I'd never been unfaithful, everything would be okay. Well, it's not. I've got as much chance of a reconciliation as you have of—of finding a Martinique oriole on St. Lucia."

"Now that would be a coup," said Peg.

"Peg, this isn't the time for birds," May scolded. "We've got to think." Thoughtfully she twirled a strand of her mauve hair. "Sex," she said.

"I beg your pardon?" said Brant.

"When a marriage goes wrong, sex is often the reason."

"We always had incendiary sex. Still would, given half a chance. Guess again."

"Money," Peg offered.

"Lots of it between our two salaries. Plus an inheritance from my father." Which he hadn't touched and never would. But he didn't have to tell them that.

"Children?" May asked.

"We never wanted them," Brant said confidently. "We both travel, it would be totally impossible to try and raise a family."

There was an awkward silence, during which May looked at Peg, who looked back at May. Then May said carefully, "I do hope we're not betraying a confidence here. But if we are, then I believe the situation calls for it—desperate times call for desperate measures. Would it have been four years ago, Peg?"

"It was the trip to Brazil, the day we saw the red-billed curassow," Peg said promptly.

"A little less than four years then. I don't remember how the conversation got around to the subject of pregnancies, but I do remember very clearly Rowan saying how much she wanted to have children, and that she didn't want to wait until her mid-thirties as so many women seem to be doing. That was the gist of it, wasn't it, Peg?"

Peg nodded. May fastened Brant with a gimlet gaze. "Perhaps Rowan never told you."

"Well," Brant said uncomfortably, feeling like a secretive bird suddenly exposed to a set of high-powered binoculars, "I guess we did talk about it. But neither of us wanted to give up our jobs."

"Yuppies," Peg said disapprovingly.

"Shush, Peg," said May.

Brant was an innately honest man. "We fought about it, actually," he muttered and took a long gulp of the smooth, dark rum he'd ordered. "Well, I suppose it wasn't really a fight, because I wouldn't even consider the prospect of having kids." He ran his fingers through his hair, thinking absently that he needed a haircut. "I told her she was being ridiculous...I even laughed at her," he finished with painful accuracy.

"There you go," said Peg, tossing back the last of her drink and plunking the glass on the counter.

May eyed him speculatively. "How old is Rowan?"

"Thirty-one."

"Time's running out."

"She wants to find someone else."

Peg said with a touch of malice, "That won't be a problem. The men will flock to her like eider ducks in springtime."

May ignored her sister. "You were away a lot during your marriage, Brant, and now you're planning to leave Rowan alone again. Tomorrow. Do you always run away from your problems?"

He felt as though she'd slapped him. "May, she told me last night the marriage is over. Over and done with. It takes two to keep a relationship going. Two, not one."

"Peg and I have known Rowan for nearly six years. She's not the kind of woman to give up so easily."

"She's had three years to do it," he growled, wishing he'd never come near the bar. Let alone the Eastern Caribbean.

"She loved you four years ago, that was very obvious to both of us. I'd be willing to bet you a trip to Borneo—which doesn't come cheap—that she still loves you."

"No takers," said Brant.

"She's like the parrots," Peg interjected. "She mates for life."

He was sick to death of all things feathered. "You're suggesting I should cancel my reservation to Toronto?"

"You've got four more islands and nine more days to win your wife back," May said vigorously.

"May," Peg remarked, "you should have been a columnist for Advice to the Lovelorn."

"Yeah," Brant said snidely, "you could set yourself up as a marriage counsellor if you ever get tired of parrots and pigeons."

"Rowan's worth any amount of advice," May retorted. "Even when it's not being asked for." And she shot Brant a sly grin.

He didn't smile back. "I've already told her I'm leaving!"

"Then tell her you're not."

"I'll see," he said tersely. Change his mind? He'd be a darned fool. Because fight or flight wasn't the real choice that was confronting him; it would more accurately be phrased as masochism versus a graceful acceptance of defeat. How could he possibly believe May's claim that Rowan still loved him? Rowan hadn't given the slightest hint of that. Instead she'd told him in no uncertain terms the marriage was over.

Could it be true he'd spent the last seven years, ever since he'd met Rowan, running away from all his problems?

If so, he wasn't much of a man. Or a husband.

May couldn't be right, not on either count. He'd been a good husband, to the very best of his ability, to a woman who had, he knew, loved him with all her heart.

So why were they divorced?

He scowled into his drink, feeling as though he were being pulled in two, and heard Peg say, "Brant Curtis, if you go back to Toronto, you're a wimp."

Her sister glared at Peg. "This is no time for insults. We have to—oh, bother, here come the rest of them. It goes without saying that we'll never breathe a word of this conversation to Rowan, Brant...I do hope they have roti on the menu. And those delicious pineapple spareribs." She added in a carrying voice, "Good evening, Karen, what a pretty dress."

Rowan was wearing shorts, Brant saw. Her legs were lightly tanned and smoothly muscled, and every bone in his body ached for her. Somehow he got through the meal by seating himself at the far end of the table from her, and through the rest of the evening by going to his room to read. The espionage novel he'd bought in Toronto didn't improve upon acquaintance. More to avoid his own thoughts than from any literary pretensions, he found himself criticizing it savagely, his pen jabbing the page of the notebook he carried with him everywhere as he annotated how he'd change plot, dialogue and character to make it a better book. Tighter. More suspense. And a lot closer to political reality.

In a sudden intuitive leap he found himself thinking about his months in Afghanistan some years ago; it'd be the perfect setting for a novel. His pen began to fly over the page as scene after scene ignited itself in his imagination, and characters leaped, seemingly fully formed, into his mind. When he finally glanced at his watch, it was one-thirty in the morning.

The opening scene of the book was so clear to him that he could hear the character's voices, smell the camel dung and feel the slide of sand under his feet. Not a bad evening's work, he thought. Not that he'd ever do anything with it. But at least it had kept him from thinking about Rowan for the better part of four hours.

As if May had indeed slapped him in the face, Brant sat straight up in his chair. Earlier this evening May had painted, in a few well-chosen words, a harsh and unflattering picture of him. All through his marriage, she'd said, he'd used his job as a way out. He'd run away from real issues. He'd laughed at them. He'd even laughed at Rowan.

He could remember the evening—only a few days after her return from Brazil, he thought sickly—when she'd raised, not for the first time, the subject of children. With a logical precision as sharp as a surgeon's scalpel he'd detailed how many times over the last year they'd both been away at the same time and how little they'd actually seen each other; he'd finished by chuckling at the absurdity of the two of them bringing a child into the world with their particular lifestyles; and then he'd taken her to bed and wooed her to compliance.

A week later he'd been assigned to check out tribal warfare in Papua New Guinea. Rowan, he realized now, had been very quiet all that week, which for her was new behavior. But he hadn't addressed her unusual constraint. Oh, no. At one level he'd been glad of it. At another he'd been too busy making meticulous preparations for his all-important job as the hot-shot, world-renowned investigative reporter, Michael Barton.

He stared at the opposite wall, where a bright band of moonlight lay, sharp-edged and cold as any scalpel. He'd been like that light. All hard edges. No give. No negotiating, he who was so skilled at negotiation in the business world. Not even any real communication, other than in bed.

His thoughts marched on. And what about this evening? He'd just spent well over four hours playing with plot, characters and dialogue, and congratulating himself because it had kept him from thinking about Rowan. Once again, he'd been running from his feelings. Different means, same end.

He realized he was cold, and got up to turn the air conditioner off. The image he'd always carried of himself as a good husband and provider was beginning to seem as shoddy and meretricious as the espionage book he'd just finished reading. He used to congratulate himself on his unswerving fidelity to Rowan, especially when he was overseas and exposed to the flagrant affairs of many of the other journalists. Despite any number of opportunities, he'd never been unfaithful to her. Never wanted to. But hadn't he cheated her in other ways?

He'd run away from conflict, and from treating her as a true equal. He'd run away from the very real commitment that a marriage requires. The only thing he hadn't run from had been sex.

Because sex had been easy.

Hastily Brant dragged the curtains shut, no longer able to tolerate that sheath of blinding light against the wall. But the darkness wasn't any better, for in it there was nowhere to hide. Tonight he'd been brought, by a series of circumstances, face to face with a man he didn't like at all, whom only a few hours ago he would vehemently have denied had anything to do with him.

A man he was starting to recognize as himself.

CHAPTER SEVEN

BRANT woke from something less than four hours sleep in a belligerent mood. He couldn't have been as oblivious to his wife's needs as May had suggested. He'd been a more than satisfactory lover to Rowan and an excellent provider. And after all, she'd known about his job before she married him.

Why did women always want to change men? Domesticate them. Turn them into tabby cats purring by the hearth instead of mountain lions prowling the high forests.

He was no tabby cat; and he was damned if he was going to cancel his flight to Toronto.

Instead he hauled on his clothes for the planned trip to the rain forest in the center of St. Lucia, and joined the others for breakfast on the patio by the limpid turquoise pool. Rowan had her back to him. He said loudly, "Good morning, Rowan. How did you sleep?"

Rowan had woken with her nerves pulled tight, like a suspension bridge over a very deep gorge. Taking her time, she looked around. "Fine, thank you, Brant," she said and let her eyes wander over his face, which showed the marks of a sleepless night. "And you?"

"Fine," he said heartily. "Going to find us a whole raft of parrots today?"

"That's my job. To find birds and keep everybody happy. Including you."

The sun gleamed in her hair like electricity and her chin was stubbornly lifted. He fought down the temptation to

91

kiss her full on the lips in front of all of them and said with lazy arrogance, "Oh, I don't think keeping me happy is part of your job description. Or ever was."

"Maybe that's just as well," she said softly. "Impossible tasks have never appealed to me."

Direct hit, he thought, and raised his glass of mango juice to her in a mocking toast. Steve said rudely, "Rowan, can you find out if there's any more papaya? Seems like they're rationing it."

"Sure," said Rowan. Brant scowled at Steve, who scowled back.

"Good morning, Brant," Peg said severely. "We should see a lot more than parrots today, as I'm sure you're aware."

He didn't have a clue what birds he was supposed to be seeing today. "I'm not always as aware as I should be," he rejoined, winking at her as he picked up a slippery slice of papaya in his fingers. "Tell me what else we're going to find."

She was now scowling at him just as Steve had, which didn't prevent her from rattling off a whole string of names just as Rowan came back from the kitchen with a new platter of papaya. He said craftily, "I'll sit next to Rowan in the van—I noticed the front had three seats. That way I can pick her brains. Okay, Rowan?"

Rowan produced a smile that felt more like the toothy grin of a shark than an expression of pleasure. "Lovely," she lied, "I'll look forward to that."

So half an hour later she was sandwiched in the front seat between the driver and Brant. She felt Brant's arm go around her shoulders; with anyone other than him she would have assumed this to be a natural enough gesture in the constricted space. As the engine roared into life she muttered, "You sure looked pleased with yourself now you know you're going back to Toronto."

He tweaked the curls on the back of her neck, his fingers lingering on her nape. "I kind of like that haircut... although it took a while to get used to it."

"Behave yourself!" she seethed. "Or are you trying to get me sent back to Toronto without a job?"

They were driving toward the capital city of Castries, the wind blowing through the open window. Brant knew he'd never see the driver again, and in the seat directly behind them Karen and Sheldon were, as usual, wrapped up in each other. He pitched his words for her ears alone. "Tell me something. Did you really want children, Rowan, that last year we were married?"

The shock ran through her body as though he had struck her, and what had started as a game with Brant suddenly changed into something of far greater significance. Her hands, he saw with a stab of compunction, were clenched in her lap where moments ago they had been loose; her cheeks had paled.

To Rowan's infinite relief a truck roared past them, and then the driver leaned out of the window to shout a greeting to two men on the side of the road. It gave her a moment's respite to recover from a question that had, in taking her by surprise, stripped her of her defenses. Her brain scurried around various answers, none of them polite, not all of them honest. Opting for at least a partial version of the truth, because Brant would be gone tomorrow, gone from her life forever, Rowan said, "Yes, I wanted children—I told you at the time that I did."

With an effort he kept his voice level. "Is that one reason you're in such an all-fired hurry to find someone else?"

"That's part of it."

"What if I told you I'd changed my mind?"

"If—it's always conditional with you, Brant. What a neat way that is to avoid commitment!"

Which, thought Brant, was basically a rephrasing of May's message, the one he'd been so busy denying ever since he'd got up this morning. He blundered on. "But what if I have changed my mind, and somehow we could work it out with our jobs so we could start a family?"

Against the arm that lay around her he felt another of those betraying shudders. She grated, "I see precious little evidence of any kind of change in you, and I'm not going to discuss this in a van full of my clients. There's no need to discuss it. You're leaving tomorrow."

"That's negotiable."

"You don't know the meaning of the word! With you, it's always been your way or the highway."

"I swear I'm not the same man who left for Colombia three years ago. I'm not just talking about having kids— I'm trying to tell you I've changed in other ways, as well."

"Then why have you been behaving like that man?" she snorted. "Stop this, Brant, I hate it." Leaning down, she pulled out her bird book. "Look up black finch, St. Lucia oriole, blue-hooded euphonia and gray trembler. That's what we're here for. This is a birding trip. Not a workshop for the repair of marriages that are beyond repair."

He couldn't pull her into his arms and kiss her until she yielded: not here. He couldn't even raise his voice to get his point across. He'd done it again, Brant realized with a sinking in his belly. Spoken without thought, chosen the worst of times and settings. He'd given more consideration to the characters who'd sprung into his imagination last night than he had to his ex-wife this morning. Why the devil did his brain cells dissolve to mush every time he came within six feet of Rowan?

He'd have to erase that word strategy from his vocabulary.

But he'd discovered one thing in the last few minutes. Rowan had indeed wanted children. She still did. She just didn't want him to be the father.

She'd changed, even if he hadn't.

The driver said amiably, "You want me to stop anywhere along the way, Rowan?"

Thankfully Rowan turned her attention to the map, pushing the backs of her hands against her knees so Brant couldn't see that her fingers were trembling. Rowan's trembler, she thought with a desperate attempt at humor, felt him remove his arm from around her shoulders and from the corner of her eye saw him open the bird book.

By tomorrow morning he'd be gone. Less than twenty-four hours. Surely she could survive one more day. She said calmly, "The only reason we might want to stop is if we pass any ponds, you never know when you're going to pick up a new shorebird."

Her voice sounded like a stranger's to her own ears, and her palms were clammy. Twenty-four hours couldn't last forever. Tomorrow, once Brant had gone, she'd be safe.

Out of danger.

As they trekked along the trail at the forest reserve Brant was rewarded by sightings of every one of the birds Rowan had mentioned. But even the euphonia, a delightful little bird feathered in green and yellow with a sky-blue topknot, didn't raise his spirits. This was the last day to be with Rowan. Like a knell, the words repeated themselves in his head. The last day, the last day...

Tomorrow he'd be back in Toronto. As soon as he landed he'd call his boss and see if the Myanmar assignment was still open. The thirty or so groups of rebels fighting it out in the forests of Burma ought to take his mind off one small group of birders on a safe little island in the Caribbean.

He'd fallen behind on the trail, not wanting the company of the others. Today, to his jaundiced eye the rain forest's dense growth epitomized nature's desperate struggle for survival: everything scrambling toward the scanty light by any means possible, like an army of guerrillas. As he came around a grove of graceful bamboo trees with their curved, hollow trunks and feathered leaves, he heard voices raised in anger, echoing his own mood, and stopped in his tracks. He couldn't deal with Steve and Natalie. Not this morning.

Then through the thicket of bamboos he heard Rowan say crisply, "I'm going to break one of my own rules here, Natalie, as well as the company's rules. It's called sticking my nose into my clients' private lives. I don't think you two would keep arguing so much if you didn't care about each other. For goodness' sake, get it together!"

"I don't—" Natalie began.

Steve said, "She isn't—"

"Shut *up!*" Rowan snapped. "Go out for dinner tonight away from the rest of us, and figure out what it is you really want from each other and how you're going to get it. That doesn't sound too difficult, does it?"

"He's a—"

"She wouldn't—"

An edge of desperation in her voice, Rowan interrupted them. "Life's too short to waste, don't you *see?* And love's not as common as you might suppose—trust me on that one. And now I'm the one who's going to shut up and not before time...isn't that a solitaire up there in that cecropia tree?"

"Oh—where's my camera?" Natalie exclaimed.

"Hanging from your shoulder," Steve said irritably. "You'd lose your head if it wasn't screwed on, Nat."

Even through the trees Brant could hear Rowan's sharp sigh of frustration. She said, "I'd better go and get Karen, she didn't see the solitaire very well the other day."

Brant stayed where he was. Rowan didn't know he'd been eavesdropping, he'd swear to it. Was she only trying to repair Steve and Natalie's relationship because her own marriage was beyond repair? Or was she trying to give them what she wanted for herself?

All thirty rebel tribes couldn't be more complicated than one red-haired woman.

For the rest of the day he watched Rowan like the proverbial hawk. She excelled at a job whose difficulties and problems she smoothed away with tact, knowledge and humor; she conjured birds out of the trees with an ease that amazed him, and she concocted another tasty picnic lunch with a minimum of fuss; she gave Steve and Natalie no more advice; and all day she treated Brant with the same unfailing courtesy with which she treated everyone else. A courtesy that made him feel about two inches tall.

This time Brant tried to plan in his mind exactly what he wanted to say to her, so he wouldn't blow it again. His first step, late in the afternoon, was to carry the cooler back to the van. Knowing he was taking a huge step into the unknown, he took Rowan by the wrist as she showed him where to stow the cooler behind the back seat. Stumbling a little, but with patent sincerity, he said, "I *have* changed, Rowan. I used to look down on your job, you're right. I'm sorry. More sorry than I can say. I'll never do that again. Because it's a very difficult job and you do it superbly."

A flash of gratification crossed her face. She stared down at the fingers clasped around her wrist, gulped, "Thank you," and then tugged herself free. "Steve," she called over her shoulder, "would you mind holding the scope while we drive? I don't want it loose in the back."

Brant found himself gawking at her back as she walked away from him. Was that it? He'd told her he was sorry and he'd complimented her on her skills, and all she could say was thank you and leave him standing here? Didn't she understand that he was changing in front of her eyes?

Didn't she care?

The day proceeded, far too quickly for Brant's liking. Natalie and Steve joined them for dinner, with May sitting between them, her mauve-haired and magisterial presence keeping them in order. Rowan was late and snagged the seat at the opposite end of the table from Brant. As coffee was being poured, the hotel manager brought her a fax; she read it, finished her coffee and disappeared. She didn't reappear.

Brant sat himself down at the bar and ordered orange juice. Time was running out. If he was going to get five minutes alone with Rowan, he'd have to do it tonight. Tomorrow morning she'd be too busy for him.

Which hurt. Hurt almost as much as her determination to ignore how he was doing his level best to change from the man he'd always been, to admit to his mistakes and make reparation.

More feelings, he thought morosely, and watched Steve sit down on the stool next to him. Under the full moon a small steel band was playing out on the patio, and several couples were dancing. Three young women who were traveling together were sitting at the other end of the bar, laughing among themselves. Steve said, "We should ask them to dance."

"Go right ahead," Brant said.

"Don't want to." Steve signaled to the bartender. "Double rum and Coke,'' he said, adding glumly, ''Never thought I'd turn down the chance to meet three new broads. They're not bad-looking, either. Especially the blonde.''

His gray eyes looked genuinely unhappy. ''Still at odds with Natalie?'' Brant asked.

''You said it.'' Steve paid for his drink and took a healthy slug. ''Do you know what she did a couple of days before we left for Grenada? Asked me to marry her.''

''What did you say?''

''I said no. That's *my* job—the guy's supposed to do the asking the way I look at it.'' He poked at an ice cube with one finger. ''She's been cranky as a dog with ticks ever since.''

Brant smothered a grin. ''Why didn't you do the asking?''

''Oh, man, what I know about marriage you could put on the back of a tick. Like nothing, you know what I mean?'' Steve took another big gulp of rum. ''You ever been married?''

''Married and divorced.''

''Hey, sorry, didn't mean to step on your toes.''

''That's okay.'' Brant hesitated fractionally. ''Rowan was my wife. We were married for four years.''

Steve's head jerked up. ''*Rowan* and you? No kidding?''

''No kidding.'' She'd kill him for telling. But after tomorrow morning, he wouldn't be here, would he?

''Jeez…so that's why there's so many vibes between the two of you. Nat picked 'em up, too. But I never figured you'd been married. What happened?''

''My job takes me all over the world at a moment's notice. Rowan travels a lot. She wanted kids. I didn't. Got so we were fighting most of the time we were together.'' Brant stirred his juice with a swizzle stick, watching the liquid swirl in the confines of the glass. "I'm starting to realize I'm a Neanderthal when it comes to feelings."

"Hey, couldn't all have been your fault."

"Well, Rowan's got a temper, for sure. As you may have noticed."

"Yeah...she doesn't fool around if she's got something on her mind." Steve looked straight at him. "You two going to get it together again?"

"Don't think so. I'm going back to Toronto tomorrow."

"Quitting?"

Steve looked so scandalized that Brant had to smile. "It takes two to tango," he said tritely. "You planning on fixing things up between you and Natalie?"

"She's gotta make the first move."

"So here we are, two guys sitting alone at the bar," Brant said dryly.

"Maybe I will ask one of 'em to dance...the blonde's sort of cute. You coming?"

Brant shook his head. "I'm too old to be putting the moves on women in a bar," he said. "Good luck."

Steve joined the three women, drinks were ordered all 'round, and Brant left the bar. The last day, he thought. The last day...

He walked back along the pathway to his room. The moon was hidden behind a cloud, blurring the shadows; the wind scythed through the leaves of the huge breadfruit tree in the center of the compound. His feet carried him past his own doorway to the room at the very end of the block, where Rowan was staying. It was in darkness. He tapped on the glass patio doors, hearing the heavy pound of his heartbeat in his ears.

Nothing happened. He tapped louder, and again got no response. Peering through the open curtains, he saw that the room was indeed empty. His disappointment was overwhelming; worse, it was laden with fear. What if he didn't get to see her before tomorrow morning? Then what would he do?

He marched to the lobby. Rowan wasn't there, or in the pool. Outside in the bar Steve was dancing with the blonde, holding her a respectable distance away from his body and looking bored to the back teeth. The beach, Brant thought. Rowan loved to swim.

If she'd gone to some of the bars and little boutiques that lined the road, he'd never find her.

He went back toward his room, through the shadows trying to find the dirt track that led to the beach. He finally located a winding pathway edged with oleander shrubs: shrubs that were deadly poisonous, he thought with a ripple of his nerves, and started along it. Then through the hiss of wind in the shrubbery he heard the crunch of footsteps coming toward him on the finely ground cinders and felt the hairs rise on the back of his neck. He stood still, waiting.

The woman who came around the corner, her shoulders brushing against the pink and white blossoms, was Rowan. She gave a gasp of shock when she saw him and he suddenly realized how threatening he must look, a black silhouette blocking the path, his height and breadth magnified by the shadows. He said quickly, "Rowan, it's me—Brant."

"B-Brant?" she quavered.

"I was looking for you, I didn't mean to scare you."

"Looking for me?"

"Yeah." Although he longed to approach her, he held his ground, all his senses on alert. "Are you okay?" he said uncertainly.

She walked right up to him, wrapped her arms around his waist and leaned all her weight on him, her head tucked under his chin, the softness of her breasts jammed against his chest. Her hair was wet; she'd obviously been swimming. With another of those judders along his nerves, Brant realized she was weeping, quietly and copiously, her tears soaking through his shirt. He put one arm around her and with his other hand lifted her face.

The moon had reappeared. In its blank white light he saw blood streaking the curve of her cheekbone. He said sharply, "Rowan—what happened?"

"I—I fell. Tripped over the curb on the way back from the beach. Oh Brant, d-don't go..."

"I'm not going anywhere—I'll take you back to your room." He held her away, running his eyes down her body; she was wearing a baggy T-shirt over a pair of shorts. "Sweetheart, your knees..."

"I don't mean now," she wailed, scrubbing at her wet cheeks and spreading more blood over her nose. "Don't go to Toronto, that's what I m-mean."

Every muscle in Brant's body went rigid. "Do you really mean that?"

"Just don't go! Please don't go..."

"If you don't want me to go to Toronto, I won't. I promise," he said forcefully. "Let me see your hands, Rowan."

Obediently she held out her palms, which were grazed and scored with dirt and blood. With a wordless exclamation Brant picked her up, holding her against his chest, and heard her falter, "Were you really looking for me?"

"Yes. I couldn't bear to leave tomorrow without one more of my jackassed attempts at reconciliation. And don't tell me I'm like a bull in a china shop when it comes to communication, I've been doing enough of a number on myself the last couple of days and yeah, I know I'm spouting clichés."

She said, the faintest thread of laughter in her voice, "In

Martinique they have these huge white bulls with long horns. One of those loose in a china shop would be a sight to behold.''

"Compared to me, it'd be a newborn calf." He emerged from the oleanders into the open, where luckily there was no one in sight. Swiftly he crossed the compound to her room. "Have you got your key?"

She pulled a cord from around her neck. Propping her against his raised knee, Brant unlocked the door and shoved it open, then carried her through, putting her down on the edge of the bed. All his movements economical, he closed the door, switched on the bedside lamp and drew the drapes shut. Only then did he really look at her.

The fieriness of temperament which had attracted him to Rowan from the start had abandoned her; she looked help-less and exhausted and very much alone. Pierced by com-passion, he said with sudden insight, "Rowan, for all our fights and love-making, I don't think we were much good at showing each other our vulnerabilities. I wasn't, I do know that much."

She was shivering. "I can't even talk about it now, I'm too tired. Just don't go to Toronto tomorrow, that's all I ask."

He knelt in front of her. "I won't. I swear I won't. I also swear I'll do my very best to figure out where we go from here. But not right now. Right now I think you should have a shower, and then I'm going to clean up your hands and knees."

"I wasn't watching where I was going, I was s-so mis-erable, and where I tripped it was all cinders on the path."

Volcanic cinders, in Brant's opinion, were probably the very worst thing you could choose if you were going to fall flat on your face. He didn't share this conclusion with Rowan. "Where's your first-aid kit?"

"Bottom left of my duffel bag."

"I'll get it. Go shower, Rowan."

She said in a rush, "I haven't got the energy to get dressed again so I'm going to put on my pajamas but I'm not—"

"The last thing we need tonight is to end up in bed together, " Brant said grimly. "We're in enough of a mess as it is...I'll try and imagine I've been reincarnated as a monk."

"Now that would be stretching the universe's powers," Rowan said with a small smile, and pushed herself up from the bed. Flinching, she added, "Hot water's going to sting like crazy, you realize that?"

He didn't offer to shower with her. He didn't offer to help her undress. You deserve a medal, buddy, he told himself, and stood up, too. "It'll relax you—you look kind of uptight."

"I could say the same of you," she remarked with another of those tiny smiles, took her pajamas from under her pillow and hobbled off to the bathroom.

Brant took out the very comprehensive first-aid kit from her duffel bag and tried not to picture Rowan's sleek body under the stream of water. She was right. He wasn't cut out to be a monk.

When she came out of the bathroom a few minutes later, her hair was a cluster of damp curls the hue of rust chrysanthemums. Her pajamas, pale green silk, consisted of a long-sleeved top and boxer shorts edged with satin, and more than hinted at her cleavage; he'd always thought her legs were exquisite. His mouth dry, Brant went into the bathroom to scrub his hands. The scent of her powder hung in the steamy air; he remembered that scent from years ago.

Rowan sat down gingerly in the room's only chair. She'd already realized that the only other choice was the bed, which wasn't really a choice at all. Through her exhaustion she was aware of the slow upwelling of a profound relief. Brant had promised he wouldn't leave tomorrow.

They had time. For what, she didn't know yet, couldn't even begin to guess. But at least when tomorrow morning came, he'd still be with her.

Brant came back from the bathroom. He was wearing cotton trousers and an open-necked blue shirt. A lock of dark hair had fallen over his forehead; he could do with a haircut. She had no idea what he was thinking, much less feeling. Not that there was anything new in that: his motivations and his demons had always been a mystery to her. He spread out some of the contents of the first-aid kit on the bed, and knelt beside her chair.

She held out her hands. Using tweezers, he picked out the fragments of cinder in her palms first, then slathered on an antibiotic ointment. Her knees were in worse shape. Despite the care he took, she couldn't always suppress her little whimpers of pain; by the time he'd finished, there was a sheen of sweat on his forehead. He taped gauze pads over the worst of the scrapes and stood up, stretching out his back. "I'm glad that's over," he said flatly.

"Me, too."

She pushed herself up, feeling her knees wobble under her. Brant announced, "Steve and I'll carry everyone's baggage tomorrow."

"Okay," Rowan said meekly.

"I don't believe it, nary an argument?" The smile died from Brant's face. Very gently he stroked her hair back from her cheek. "I don't know what we're going to do, or what we need to say to each other in the next few days, Rowan. If you want the truth, whenever I'm around you I'm scared out of what few wits I seem to possess."

He didn't look scared. He looked tender and solicitous,

the way he'd looked with Gabrielle that awful day at the hospital. She bit her lip. "I don't know how to read you...I don't think I ever have."

He was slowly and rhythmically caressing her cheekbone, not meeting her eyes; the lamplight gleamed in the dusting of gray in his hair, shadowing the new lines in his face. Her heart caught in her breast; he could so easily not have come back from Colombia. Oddly, there was nothing sexual in his caress, and Rowan was suddenly, fiercely glad of this. Over the years she'd come to distrust the way their bodies could fuse so ardently while the rest of their lives remained so far apart.

He said with the same slowness, "The fact that you want me to stay here and that I want to stay—it's like a huge weight's been lifted from my shoulders. As though I've been released from prison for the second time 'round. Whatever's going on, we're in it together." He lifted his blue eyes, which blazed with pent-up emotion. "You have no idea how good that feels."

Tears pricked at her lids. "Yes, I do," she said softly, and did what she'd been wanting to do ever since he'd knelt by her chair a few minutes ago. With a tenderness that felt as deep as the sea, she stroked the dark lock of hair back from his forehead and smiled up at him. "I've felt very much alone the last three years," she confessed. "And it's like a small miracle that I'm actually saying that to you."

Brant took her in his arms, holding her wordlessly while time seemed to stop and the tension that drove him so mercilessly and so constantly slackened its grip. Then, gradually, he became aware of other, more earthy sensations: the warmth of her body, the lissome curve of her spine and the scent of her skin. He edged away from her. "I'd better go."

Rowan took her courage in her hands. "Do you know what I want to say?" she whispered. "Stay with me, Brant, sleep with me, hold me in your arms the night through so I won't be alone...I've been lonely for so long, it sometimes feels like forever. But I'm not going to say it. Maybe I'm scared to, scared that we'll just fall back into all the old patterns."

Brant never cried. He couldn't start now. He said huskily, "You're so wise and brave and beautiful...and, dammit, you're right, as well. We shouldn't get into bed together, not yet." He paused. "Just as long as you know that I want to."

She chuckled. "Now that's one thing I've never doubted."

He chucked her under the chin, knowing he could leave now that she was laughing. "I'll see you in the morning. The flight's not that early for once."

"We can sleep in until seven o'clock, how decadent that sounds...good night, Brant." Good night, she thought with deep thankfulness. Not goodbye.

He leaned over and brushed his mouth to hers, then left her room. The moon was now entangled in the tall branches of the breadfruit tree; the cool, luminous night enfolded Brant in its arms, as Rowan had enfolded him in hers.

He felt happy.

For the first time in years, he felt happy.

CHAPTER EIGHT

BRANT woke happy the next morning. Happy, and in a physical condition such that had Rowan been there, she'd have been in no doubt as to his intentions.

She'd be in his bed again, and soon. He knew it.

They'd figure out what had gone wrong with the marriage. If they made it a joint effort, it shouldn't be too difficult. Although the thought of raising children made him break into a cold sweat.

But he wasn't going to think about that today. They both needed a respite from the last few days, from the anger, confusion and unhappiness that had traveled with them ever since she'd walked up to him in the airport in Grenada.

He got out of bed and headed for the shower, whistling. On his way to breakfast he met up with Steve and said cheerfully, "Good morning."

Steve growled, "You think there'd be two seats on that flight to Toronto? Nat saw me dancing with the blonde."

"But you looked bored to tears."

"The woman I was dating before Nat was blonde. She thinks I've got a thing about 'em."

"You can have my seat. I'm not going."

Steve brightened minimally. "You're not? Hey, man, that's great. What happened?"

"Rowan didn't want me to leave any more than I wanted to. Luckily we discovered this before I got on the plane. But you don't really want to fly out of here, Steve—why don't you just tell Natalie you're sorry and see what happens?"

"In the mood she's in? No way."

If Steve hadn't looked so unhappy, Brant might have lost patience. But Brant knew what that kind of unhappiness felt like. "Hang in there," he said. "Not that I know what makes women tick any more than you do."

"Four years of marriage to a neat gal like Rowan and you still don't know?" Steve said tactlessly.

"I never gave my marriage priority," Brant admitted. "My job was always more important."

"Women don't like that."

"They've got a point, wouldn't you say?"

With a certain self-righteousness Steve replied, "I'd rather be windsurfing or scuba diving right now. But I'm trailing around the countryside looking at birds because Nat likes to photograph 'em. You can't say I'm not putting her first."

"Maybe you'd be better off windsurfing and letting her do the photography…then you'd both be doing what you want to do, and you could be together the rest of the time."

Steve looked unconvinced. "How am I going to suggest that to her when she won't even talk to me?"

"Just do it and see what happens…oh, good morning, Rowan."

Rowan said with an endearing touch of shyness, "Hi, Brant. Steve, how are you?"

"Going to grab me a couple of croissants before Sheldon hogs the lot," Steve said, and marched off toward the dining room.

"How are your knees?" Brant asked.

"They've been better. But we're not doing much hiking today."

"Sleep well?" He let his eyes wander over her face. "You look very beautiful, my darling."

She blushed, sneaked a quick look around and kissed him

full on the mouth, a kiss whose brevity didn't negate its passion. Then she gabbled, "We've got an awful lot of talking to do, we mustn't forget that."

"How about we give it a rest today? I'm just so god-damned glad I'm not getting on that plane to Toronto. .let's not worry about the future or dig up the past, not today. *Carpe diem* and all that."

"Sounds like a plan."

He laughed, the carefree laugh of a much younger man. "It's probably just as well we'll be chaperoned all day by six eagle-eyed birders—I'm not feeling at all monkish."

"I'll take that as a compliment."

"So you should."

Rowan glanced past his shoulder. "Speaking of eagles...good morning, Peg. Good morning, May."

Brant turned. "I was just telling Rowan how much I'm looking forward to Martinique and Guadeloupe," he said easily; the last time he'd talked to them he'd been hell-bent on going back to Toronto. "It'll give me the chance to brush up on my French."

"The language of love," Peg said mistily.

"One of the Romance languages," May said.

"It never hurts to brush up on a language you haven't been using," Peg added with a touch of severity.

"One can always improve one's vocabulary and one's usage," said her sister. "Wouldn't you agree, Brant?"

"I'm sure you're right," Brant replied, wanting nothing more than to change the subject. "Shall we go to break-fast?"

"We'll get the white-breasted thrasher in Martinique," Peg said happily, striding toward the dining room.

"And the oriole, don't forget the oriole," May said.

"An early start tomorrow," her sister remarked. "I'm not much for all this sleeping in."

It was seven-twenty in the morning. "Positively sloth-
ful," Brant said, and pulled out two chairs, one for Rowan
and one for himself. Sheldon and Karen looked like a couple who'd spent the night making very satisfactory love,
while Natalie, beneath a layer of makeup, looked as though
she were simmering with things unsaid; Brant wouldn't
have wanted to be Steve. The whole group showed such
solicitude for Rowan's scraped hands that he was touched.

At the airport he canceled his flight to Toronto, and
nabbed the seat next to Rowan on the plane. It was a small
plane; he took great pleasure in the rub of her thigh against
his and in watching the little vein pulse in the hollow of
her wrist. He felt more than happy. He felt exuberant, as
though he could have lifted the plane from the tarmac sin-
gle-handedly.

They flew over a turquoise sea with its curved reefs and
its white triangles of sailboats, and then over the red roofs
and dry hills of Martinique. That afternoon they drove to a
beach at the very south of the island, where Brant in his
binoculars saw a yellow warbler whose feathers were
brighter than the sun and whose confiding dark eyes seemed
to look right at him; again he felt that unaccustomed rush
of pleasure in the natural world.

A flock of tropic birds was circling overhead, with their
arched wings and streamered tails, dazzlingly white against
the sky. He gazed at them for a long time, long after the
rest of the group had moved on, and knew he wanted for
himself and for Rowan that grace and ease, that sense of
being so much at home with each other and with the wild
and constant winds of the sea.

All that afternoon Rowan found herself watching Brant. He
looked like a different man today, she thought humbly, his
face gentled and relaxed, happy in a way she could scarcely

remember. Too happy? For after all, nothing was settled, nothing was dealt with, and underneath her own deep relief that he hadn't left for Toronto was a burgeoning fear.

Was Brant changing, as he claimed he was? Could they rebuild a marriage different in reality as well as in spirit from their previous one? She knew she was willing to work very hard to achieve that. But she couldn't do it alone. Furthermore, to do so, she would have to share with him that longtime secret which was hers alone, yet which concerned him at the deepest of levels; it was a prospect she dreaded.

"Least sandpiper!" Peg hollered, and hastily Rowan dragged her attention back to her job. When they returned to the hotel she was almost glad she and her driver had groceries and other errands to do. Afterward she showered, put on a calf-length sundress that hid the deplorable state of her knees, and wandered down to the beach.

Steve and Brant were windsurfing, both of them well offshore where the breeze skimmed their boards over the waves. Natalie was stretched out on a beach chair; she was wearing a shiny bronze bikini, her face inscrutable behind huge sunglasses. "Hi, Natalie," Rowan said, "do you mind if I join you?"

"Go right ahead. Rowan, why are men such creeps?"

Rowan sat down, careful not to bend her knees too much. "Men identify with their jobs, women with their relationships," she said promptly, and wondered from what magazine article she'd gleaned that gem of wisdom. It had, from her own experience, the ring of truth.

"Look at the two of them out there, happy as pigs in…well, happy. Steve'd much rather be surfing than birding. He only came along to keep me happy."

Natalie's red mouth was drooping. "He's not exactly succeeding, is he?" Rowan said gently.

"Are you and Brant a number?"

"No…yes…oh, I don't know," Rowan said in exasperation.

"See what I mean? They're dorks."

Both men were now racing at an angle toward the beach. The muscles of Brant's shoulders and thighs were sharply delineated, his whole body taut as an athlete's: strain gracefully borne, thought Rowan, all his strength and nerve focused on the task at hand. As he passed dangerously close to some rocks, she heard him laugh in exhilaration. His board was carving a bow wave from the blue water; perfectly balanced, he raced toward the sand, and at the last minute sank into the sea. Only then did he see her.

He waved, hauled his board partway on the beach and ran toward her, shaking the water from his hair. The sun gleamed on his wet body and she wanted him so badly she could scarcely breathe. He said, still laughing, "I won—right?"

She said primly, "A tie. Wasn't it, Natalie?"

"Nah…Steve won," Natalie said.

Steve had stayed in the water, and was towing his board around for another run. Brant yelled, "Be right there," and said awkwardly, "He misses you, Natalie."

"So let him tell me—he's got a big enough mouth."

Rowan sighed. "Dinner in half an hour, Brant."

He leaned down and gave her a very explicit kiss. "One more run. Save me the seat next to you."

As he jogged back down the sand, Rowan, left gaping like a stranded fish, sputtered, "They're not only creeps, they're arrogant and insufferable creeps and why can't we live without them?"

"You find the answer to that one, you'd be a rich woman," Natalie said. "Still, Brant seems an okay feller.

Maybe you should give him half a chance instead of freezing him out every time he comes near you.''

"This trip is more like a prolonged singles weekend than an ornithological field trip! I'm going to have a drink, I'll see you at dinner.'' And Rowan made good her escape.

But as she walked toward the dining room to check on their dinner reservation, she was thinking hard. There was no give with Natalie and Steve; each of them wanted the other to make the first move and was prepared to wait—and suffer—until that happened. Brant and I aren't like that, not anymore, thought Rowan with a tinge of smugness. We're meeting each other halfway. How else can we repair all the damage that our marriage caused? We haven't got the time for games.

After dinner, served late and with a bewildering array of courses, Brant escorted Rowan back to her room. In the shadow of some hibiscus shrubs he kissed her good night with evident restraint. Rowan, who wanted more, pulled his head down and ran her tongue along his upper lip. He then kissed her until their combined heartbeats sounded like a tattoo and her inability to stand had nothing to do with the scrapes on her knees. She gasped, "I shouldn't have done that, Brant...encouraged you like that, I mean...I'm sorry.''

"I don't know how I can be around you for the rest of the week and not make love to you," he groaned, nuzzling her throat, his hands sliding down her bare arms to clasp her waist.

"We've got to talk first," she said frantically. What a hypocrite she was, when all she wanted to do was tear the clothes from his body and make love to him the night through.

Just as well it was still the wrong time of the month. Or she'd be in deep trouble.

"Tomorrow evening," he grated. "We'll go for a walk along the beach away from the rest of them and try and figure out where we're going from here."

Which gave her exactly twenty-four hours to work out what she had to say. How to tell him what had happened that dreadful day she got the news he'd been abducted.

It didn't sound like nearly long enough.

The next morning Brant watched Rowan locate three of the rare white-breasted thrashers in the scrub forest on Presqu'ile de la Caravelle; he had to commend her patience, strategy and persistence. Unfortunately she also located a disheartening number of the mongoose that preyed on the thrashers. They then drove to a rain forest trail for the oriole. Brant wasn't feeling nearly as relaxed today. Despite the lack of sex, yesterday had been like a honeymoon. But today he had to convince Rowan to come back to him; and once again, his much-vaunted intelligence seemed to have deserted him. The fact that he craved her body wouldn't do him any good. The thought of starting a family panicked him. And she hated his job. None of this did much for his confidence that he could undo the damage of their divorce.

As the group picnicked under some tall pines, he fed most of his lunch to a stray cat, who then curled up in the grass and went to sleep; he envied its ability to be so unconcerned about the future. Rowan, he noticed, had a tendency to avoid his gaze. Unless he was very much mistaken, she was in as much of a funk as he was. This didn't comfort him in the slightest.

He was sure of only one thing. He wanted her back.

After lunch they stopped along the shore a few times to check out mangrove swamps. At the last stop Brant wandered away from the rest of them, and was rewarded by the sight of a plumed night heron fishing in the brackish waters of the swamp. He watched it for a long time, its single-minded concentration on the matter of food somehow encouraging him that if he only wanted Rowan enough, everything would turn out for the best. He had to trust himself, he thought. Himself, and her.

The alternative, that they would remain forever alienated, was insupportable.

Rowan had seen Brant disappear down the shore; she would have liked to do the same, because under her surface efficiency and good manners she was a mass of jangled nerves. In less than five hours her whole future would be decided, and she still had no idea what she was going to say.

She knew what she wanted: the same man and a different marriage.

In the swamp they found two kinds of egrets and a handsome green heron, and she was about to lead the birders back to the van when Natalie said, "Just a sec. I haven't gotten a photo of a cattle egret sitting on a cow yet—there's a field full of neat white cows just beyond those trees."

She took off at a fast clip. The wind from the sea was hot, the humidity stifling, and even May and Peg looked a little wilted. Rowan said, "I'll follow her, I guess...I'd still love to find a little egret."

"We'll all go," Peg said stoutly.

"Karen's tired," Sheldon said, "we'll stay here."

"If Brant comes back, tell him where we are," Rowan said, and headed after Natalie, Steve right behind her.

The grass was crisp and brown underfoot. As they left the mangroves behind, to her left Rowan heard the plaintive lowing of a cow. Then, splitting the still air like the swish of a machete, Natalie screamed.

For an instant Rowan was frozen in her tracks, the sun beating on her bare arms. Steve said, "What the hell—"

and started to run through the last of the trees, brushing aside branches and leaping over roots.

Rowan dropped the scope, hauled off her heavy haversack and asked May to watch them. Then she took off after him, racing across the dusty ground, ignoring the pain in her knees as that terrified scream echoed in her ears. She reached the barbed-wire fence around the field in time to see Steve clamber over it and a flock of cattle egrets take to the air at the far end of the field where a herd of cows grazed peacefully; and then she saw why Natalie had screamed.

Her camera around her neck, Natalie was edging backward from a very large cream-colored bull, talking to it in a high-pitched voice that at any other time might have been funny. The bull looked more interested in her than aggressive; but bulls, in Rowan's opinion, were not the most trustworthy of creatures.

Steve said in a loud voice, "Nat, as soon as I distract it, head for the fence." Then he started jumping up and down, yelling obscenities at the top of his voice.

The bull swung its massive head around, pawing at the ground with one large hoof. Natalie looked back over her shoulder, her cheeks as white as the feathers of any egret, and speeded up her retreat. The bull took one step after her, and she whimpered with fear. Then Steve picked up a rock and fired it at the bull. As the rock bounced off its flank, it snorted and turned its full attention to Steve.

Natalie was only a few feet from the fence. Rowan parted the strands, saying urgently, "This way, Natalie, not much further."

With another hunted look over her shoulder, Natalie stumbled toward the fence and scrambled through it; when two wire spikes caught in her shirt, she gave an exclamation of sheer panic. "Hold still," Rowan ordered, and carefully pulled the sharp wire from the cotton fabric. "There, you're okay now," she said.

Natalie grabbed her, burying her face in Rowan's shoulder; she was quivering all over. "How was I to know it was a bull?" she stuttered. "I was b-brought up in Boston."

Rowan patted her soothingly on the shoulder, decided lessons on basic anatomy could wait for another time, and with a flare of fear saw that the bull was advancing on Steve. She shouted, "Steve, Natalie's safe...get back here. Fast!"

Natalie's head reared up. "Steve?" she croaked. "Omigod, Steve—"

As she lunged for the fence, Rowan held on to her with all her strength. "He'll be fine," she cried, "you can't go back in there," and saw Steve begin to run toward the fence.

The bull started after him, breaking into a graceless canter. From behind her Rowan heard the pound of steps through the grass, and as though it were happening in slow motion watched Brant shuck off his haversack, dump it on the ground and vault the fence in a single agile flow of movement. He stooped and flung a sharp-edged rock at the bull.

The bull bellowed in surprise and wheeled to this new threat. Brant tore at the buttons on his shirt and hauled it from his back, waving it provocatively to one side of his body. He was, Rowan saw with a sick lurch of her heart, laughing.

Steve had reached the barbed-wire fence. He shoved himself through it and stumbled over to Rowan, his eyes only on Natalie. "Are you okay, Nat?" he demanded.

Natalie threw herself from Rowan's arms into Steve's, grabbing on to him as though she'd never let go. "That was so brave of you," she wailed. "Oh, Steve, I do love you."

"I love you, too," Steve muttered. "Sorry I've been such a jerk."

"Not half as dumb as I've been," Natalie said with a beatific smile, wriggled her hips against his and kissed him very thoroughly.

Rowan tore her eyes away. The bull was charging Brant.

Her breath was stuck in her throat and every muscle was paralyzed with terror. The whole world had narrowed to a man and an animal. A man who meant more to her than all the world. Like a woman turned to stone she waited for the inevitable and unequal collision; for Brant to be broken like a doll, crushed and gored in front of her eyes.

Brant shook the shirt so it billowed in the sea breeze and at the very last moment threw himself sideways. The sleeve caught in the bull's horns and ripped free, the sound shockingly loud through the thud of its hooves and the crunch of dirt. The bull tossed its head, infuriated by the scrap of fabric that blocked its vision, and swerved to charge again.

Brant had taken those few precious seconds to get closer to the fence. But not close enough, Rowan saw with an ugly lurch of her heart. Then, in a surge of rage that momentarily dispelled fear and that horrified her with its primitive force, she saw that he was still laughing, his teeth gleaming in his tanned face, his chest slick with sweat.

He was enjoying himself.

It was what had driven them apart, this deep need of his for danger, this hunger to live on the edge. She'd never been able to compete with it. Never.

In a reckless and mocking parody of a bullfighter, Brant swirled the shirt through the air and pivoted to one side. The bull tried to snag the shirt on its horns, but mysteriously the shirt was somewhere else. The bull gave another deep bellow, its great hooves churning up the dust as it, like Brant, pivoted.

It's a dance, thought Rowan dizzily. A dance with danger. A dance with death. That's what drives Brant.

I can't stand to go through this again.

Her fists were bunched at her sides, her nails digging into her scraped palms; dimly she was aware that her knees were bleeding from her frantic run to get to the field. Once more the bull charged, and this time Brant, in a split-second move that was perfectly judged, wrapped his shirt over the wickedly pointed horns, temporarily blinding the animal.

Brant seized his chance, racing for the fence and again vaulting over it with a lithe grace. Snorting ferociously, the bull scraped its horns in the dirt, reducing the shirt to a tangle of shredded fabric.

It could have been Brant, Rowan thought, and wondered if she was going to be sick.

She couldn't be. Not in front of everyone.

Steve and Natalie disentangled themselves long enough for Natalie to gush, "That was wonderful, Brant," and for Steve to say, "Yeah…thanks, man—you got me out of a tight spot."

"You're welcome," Brant panted, wiping the sweat from his forehead with the back of his hand.

He felt great, all his senses alert, his whole body alive with the rush of adrenaline. Then he looked over at the red-haired woman standing stock-still by the fence. Her cheeks were ashen-pale and there was something in her face that instantly banished his euphoria. He took two quick strides toward her, grabbing her by the elbow. "Rowan, you okay?"

She couldn't tell him what she was feeling. Not now, not in front of Natalie, Steve, Peg and May; for the two elderly women had by now arrived on the scene. With a monumental effort Rowan swallowed a turmoil of emotion that would consume her should she give it voice, and said stonily, "I'm fine. Shall we go back to the van? Thanks for looking after the scope, Peg—and my haversack, May."

"Brant, we thought you were going to be killed," Peg exclaimed.

"Right in front of us," May shuddered.

"Not a chance," Brant said with a cheerfulness that grated on Rowan's nerves. "Here, Peg, let me carry the scope."

"You were *very* brave," Peg said. "Wasn't he, Rowan?"

"Very," Rowan said in the same stony voice, and pulled her elbow free as Peg passed Brant the scope.

After one look at Rowan's face, May tucked her arm in her sister's and urged her in the direction of the van; Steve and Natalie were already heading that way, their arms around each other. Brant fell into step beside Rowan. He said noncommittally, "What was Steve doing in a field with a bull?"

"Rescuing Natalie who was taking a photo of an egret and didn't seem to realize that the cow it was sitting on was a bull."

"What's up, Rowan?" he went on with menacing softness. "You look like you're going to explode."

She glared into his brilliant blue irises. "It'll keep," she snapped. "Until tonight. Seeing as how I'd like to hold on to my job, it wouldn't be smart of me to stage a screaming match in front of my clients. Plus I prefer to keep my private life private. Weird of me, but there you are."

He didn't think it was the time to tell her that May, Peg and Steve all knew that he and Rowan had been married. She'd cut his throat from ear to ear by the look of her.

"Well, at least Nat and Steve seem to have mended their differences," he said.

"Hurray for them."

"Bully for them," he grinned, raising one brow.

"Cute," she seethed. "Real cute. Put on a T-shirt or you'll get sunburn."

"Don't tell me what to do, my darling Rowan."

"Don't call me darling!"

"Why did I ever think the Caribbean would be dull?" Brant drawled, putting down the scope and his haversack on the grass and pulling out a T-shirt.

As he raised his arms to pull it over his head, Rowan dragged her eyes away from his lean rib cage, where sun and shadow played over sinew and bone. The van was in sight now, the driver patiently sitting in the shade waiting for them. Karen and Sheldon were cuddled together on the beach, as close as the two halves of a shell, while Natalie and Steve were in a Hollywood clinch against a tree. She'd like to chuck the whole bunch of them, scope and all, into the sea and drive off without them, Rowan thought vengefully.

She couldn't do that. She needed her salary. She called out, "Let's head back to the hotel, I'm sure everyone's ready for a swim and a cool drink after that bit of excitement."

Bit of excitement? Who was she kidding? Death knell to her hopes for a different marriage was more like it.

The wind stirred her hair as they left the beach and drove down the road past a field of sugarcanes; and belatedly Rowan realized why she'd been trying so hard to hold on to her rage.

Because beneath it lay despair. Brant hadn't changed. Couldn't change. So tonight she'd be defeated before she even opened her mouth.

CHAPTER NINE

AT NINE that night Brant crossed the quadrangle toward Rowan's room. He had on his best blue shirt and new cotton trousers, and he'd showered, shaved and brushed his hair: just as though he were an adolescent on his first date. But he didn't feel like an adolescent. He felt like a grown man on a hazardous assignment, who could be walking into an ambush over ground sown with land mines.

And his life depended on how he handled this particular assignment.

He raised his fist and tapped on the door of her room. Rowan opened it immediately, as if she'd been waiting on the other side. She was wearing the same sundress she'd worn for dinner, with a lacy shawl thrown over her shoulders, and she looked like a woman standing in front of a firing squad. Unsmilingly she said, "Where are we going?"

Like a good strategist, he'd already scouted out the territory. "There are some rocks at the far end of the beach beyond the pier, why don't we sit there?"

Side by side they walked down the path. Brant could think of nothing to say; just like a goddamned adolescent, he thought in exasperation. "How are your knees?" he asked.

"No sign of infection. Thanks," she added as an afterthought.

"Good." He racked his brains. "We go to Dominica tomorrow?"

"Yes. It's my favorite of all the islands, it's not developed very much and the birds are wonderful. We do a boat trip there, too, that's always fun.''

He asked a couple of questions, she answered them and by then they'd reached the beach. It was deserted; music from the disco drifted over the water, while the moon had shrunk a little, its pale light shimmering on the waves. Brant took Rowan's elbow as they started over the sand. She flinched from his touch, and his nerves tightened another notch. "This isn't a seduction scene," he said.

"I never thought it was."

Her voice was a cold as the moonlight. They walked past the stone jetty to the rocks that lay beyond it, where the dark fronds of a palm grove rustled to themselves. Rowan turned to face him, thrusting her hands in the pockets of her dress. Like an adversary, Brant thought. Not like a woman intent on reconciliation.

Instantly she went on the attack, her words falling over themselves. "You *had* to do that this afternoon, didn't you? Play with that bull as though it were a stuffed teddy bear and not an animal that could have killed you."

"I was never in any real danger."

"If you'd tripped and fallen, it would have gored you the way it ripped your shirt to pieces." Her voice was shaking. "You haven't changed. You can't, you don't know how."

"What did you want me to do? Leave Steve in the field to be gored instead?"

"You enjoyed it!"

"So what?"

Rowan jammed her fists still deeper in her pockets, pulling her dress tight over her breasts, and said raggedly, "I love you and I want to live with you again, but—"

"You *love* me?"

She said blankly, "Well, yes. Of course. Why else do you think I'm here?"

"Despite everything, you still love me?"

"Don't you love me?" she asked in a hostile voice.

"Sure I do," Brant answered in a dazed voice, and knew he'd spoken the literal truth. A truth he'd had to travel twenty-five hundred miles to discover. "That was one more reason why I wasn't even tempted to sleep with Gabrielle, how could I make love to her when I love you with all my heart?"

Love. Present tense.

If, after this declaration, Brant had expected Rowan to fall into his arms as easily as a ripe coconut falls from a palm tree, he was soon disillusioned. She said, "I want you to quit your job."

The breath hissed between his teeth. Twice in less than a minute she'd outflanked him. Taken him completely by surprise. You're losing your touch, Brant, old man. "Are you serious?" he said. She nodded. "Give it up altogether?"

"Yes."

"You don't ask much, do you? Why do you want me to quit my job, Rowan?"

"I can't imagine you even have to ask that question."

"I am asking it," he said, holding tight to his temper.

She tossed her head. "You've got a choice. You can live with me and have a different job or you can keep the one you've got and stay divorced."

"I never thought blackmail was one of your talents," he said unpleasantly.

Her head jerked up, her nostrils flared. "Maybe we should quit right here—the shortest reconciliation on record," she said bitterly. "Because I'm not going to budge on this one, Brant. I don't know how to get through to you the cost of your job to me. In loneliness. Constant anxiety. Outright terror when I pick up the newspaper and see that the latest coup is in the place you flew into three days ago. I can't do it anymore! I won't do it anymore."

"But I—"

"You saw how I looked this afternoon by the time you got out of that field! Try stretching that out over two weeks, or a month, or six weeks...however long your assignment lasts. I can't take it anymore. Lying awake night after night worrying about you. Knowing there's nothing I can do to keep you safe. Knowing I'm not as important to you as your job." She scuffed at the sand with the toe of her sandal, her head downbent. "I'm tired of being second on the list."

"I always came back," he said forcefully. "I never took unnecessary risks, and I always knew what I was doing."

"Then why were you abducted?"

"That was sheer bad luck," he said impatiently.

"No, it wasn't! You're the one who'd put yourself in the situation to start with."

"So once in eleven years at that job I got into trouble," he said furiously. "I'd call that a pretty good record."

The words tumbled from Rowan's lips. "Perhaps it's my fault you've never understood how badly your job affected me. What you said a couple of days ago about not sharing our vulnerabilities— I was guilty of that, too. Before you left on an assignment I'd try not to show you how much I dreaded you going, I think I was afraid it might jinx you so you'd never come back." Her voice was shaking again. "And then when you came back, we'd fall into bed and it would all be forgotten. Until next time."

She suddenly gripped his bare forearm with one hand. "At the end I tried to tell you, before you left for Colombia. But you weren't listening, were you? And let me tell you something else. That eight months was the worst time of my whole life. Eight months of wondering if I was already a widow. If I'd ever find out what had happened to you or if you'd just disappear without a trace. No news, no body, nothing. It was so horrible... Oh, Brant, don't you *see?* I can't live like that anymore.''

Staring down at her fingers, he said, ''Where's your wedding ring?''

''Home,'' she said shortly. ''In the drawer.''

''I'd be nothing without my job,'' he said with raw honesty. ''It's what I do.''

She said steadily, ''I don't believe that. You're much bigger than your job.''

''I've done a lot of good over the years.''

''Of course you have! Don't think I don't know that.'' Her smile was wry. ''I just need you to be a different kind of hero, that's all.''

He repeated the one thing he was sure of in this whole mess. ''You've never stopped loving me.''

''I don't know how.''

''And you were never unfaithful to me.''

''Not even an issue.''

Shaken to the depths of his being, Brant put his arms around her and rested his cheek on her hair. ''I love you, too, Rowan,'' he said hoarsely. ''We're bound together, you and I...''

Her voice smothered in his chest, she mumbled, ''I don't think we ever really were divorced.''

So Gabrielle had been right: some divorces weren't worth the paper they were written on. But Brant didn't want to think about Gabrielle. Rather, he wanted to savor the wonder of holding Rowan close again. Her body felt absolutely right in his arms; it was an embrace, he thought humbly, that went far beyond the sexual. He said, ''This is what I want. You. But I don't have a clue how to go about getting it.''

Her arms were snug around his waist; he could hear the small, steady thud of her heartbeat against his chest. She said so quietly he could barely hear her, ''When you were away, the loneliness was the worst. Waking in the night to an empty bed, coming home from one of my trips to an empty apartment, going to the market on Saturday morning on my own, going to the movies and seeing people in couples…oh, God, how I hated the loneliness.'' She lifted her head. ''I'm no saint, Brant. Now that I look back, I think I lost my temper all over the place and at the drop of a hat instead of trying to make you understand how difficult it was without you. In the long run, losing my cool didn't really accomplish very much.''

''Whereas I'd just go away on another assignment. Run away. Because that's what it was.''

Her smile was troubled. ''Hindsight's great stuff, isn't it?''

But where do we go from here? Brant said helplessly, ''I love my job, Rowan.'' As if a tape deck had been turned on, into his brain clicked Gabrielle's words the evening she'd told him about this trip. *I've watched you the last two years. You've been acting like a man demented. Like a man who couldn't care less if he got himself killed.* Was that the attitude of someone who loved his job? Or had he been using his job to kill the pain of Rowan's absence?

Rowan said trenchantly, ''Maybe you should try and figure out why you're in love with danger. Maybe she's been your real mistress all these years.''

He couldn't have stopped the tremor that ran through his body. *In love with danger…* That, he knew, went back to a five-year-old boy whose mother had died and whose father had taken over his upbringing. "You'll be recommending a therapist next," he said nastily.

"I hit home there, didn't I?"

Another nasty retort was on the tip of his tongue. Brant bit it back. The stakes were too high to indulge in name-calling. Much too high. His mouth dry, he said, "I've never talked much about my father...never wanted to."

"Perhaps it's time," she said.

His throat closed. "If I quit my job, what else would I do?"

She was frowning in thought. "All these years I wonder if somehow you've been living your father's life—instead of your own."

"I don't want to talk about him!"

"Sooner or later you'll have to."

With unwilling admiration Brant said, "You don't quit easy, do you?"

"Not where you're concerned," she said pertly. "But don't let it go to your head."

He kissed the tip of her nose. "Or to any other parts of my anatomy."

She nuzzled his breastbone in a gesture that tore at his heart, so familiar was it, and so deeply missed. "We shouldn't get into bed with each other, not yet," she said.

The words were dragged from him. "You want children."

This time it was she who quivered as though he'd struck her. "Yes," she whispered. "Your children, Brant."

He tried it out on his tongue. "Our children."

A single tear hung on her lashes. "I've got—" But then she broke off, biting her lip, her face anguished.

"Sweetheart, what's wrong?"

She shook her head; the muscles in her throat moved as

she swallowed. "I just don't want to wait any longer, I'm thirty-one years old," she said.

He knew in his gut that she'd been about to say something different. Later, he thought, one thing at a time; and again tried to be as honest as he knew how. "I'm scared to death of having kids."

"I think your father has a heck of a lot to answer for!"

She looked very militant. He'd like to have seen Rowan and his father face to face, it would have been a confrontation worth witnessing; Douglas Curtis, however, had died two years before Brant met Rowan. "Do you think I'd be any good as a father?"

"If you gave yourself half a chance, I think you'd be a wonderful father."

It was the third time she'd knocked him off balance. He had none of her certitude about himself in the role of father. None at all. Seeking refuge in practicalities, he asked, "What would I do if I quit my job?"

"I've thought about that quite a bit. You could make a list of all your skills, see what's marketable…you're a very smart man, there's lots you could do. You could even start your own company, taking people to out-of-the-way places." She looked at him through her lashes. "Just don't include Colombia."

He burst out, "If I quit my job and then it didn't work out between you and me—I'd have nothing left."

She winced. "If we both want it to work out, it will."

Brant was quite astute enough to pick up the undercurrent of doubt in her voice. "What about your job? You travel, too. You can't very well go careering around the rain forest if you're seven months pregnant."

"I'd cut back on the number of trips I take. And my company gives maternity leave."

Her head was held high. But in the pallid moonlight he

could see the lines of strain around her mouth and the shadows under her eyes. "Why don't you sit down for a minute?" he said. "You look tired out."

As she turned, Rowan stumbled over a rock. Losing her balance, she banged her knee against the jagged edge of a big boulder. She gave a yelp of pain, put out a hand to support herself, scraped her sore palm and gave another pained yelp. Brant reached her in one quick stride and eased her down on the boulder. "Let me see your knee."

She lifted her skirt. The blood trickling down her shin was black as ink. He said, "God, sweetheart, your knee's a mess."

"When Natalie screamed this afternoon, I took off like a bullet out of a gun. That kind of wrecked it."

"We'd better go back...I'll put some more ointment on."

Rowan took him by the wrist. "Are we going to be okay?" she blurted.

He lifted her to her feet, wondering how he'd existed for over three years without being able to touch her and hold her in his arms. "We've got to be," he said huskily. "Because I can't live without you. You were never second, Rowan. I just behaved as though you were, and for that I deserve to be horsewhipped through three counties."

"You really *are* sorry..."

"Sorry—that's one hell of a wishy-washy word for the way I'm feeling. But yeah, that's what I'm saying."

"You've got a lot of feelings, Brant Curtis," Rowan said in a small voice. "You've just got to learn to let them out more often."

"Plus find a new job and raise a passel of kids," Brant said wryly. "Anything else you can add to the list?"

She gave a sudden delightful laugh. "Maybe somewhere

in there you should marry me again. For the sake of the children, you understand.''

"For our sake," he said fiercely, and kissed her with all the love that had been locked inside him for so long. Too long. She kissed him back with all her old tempestuousness; they were both trembling when he finally released her. She whispered, "I think I'd better look after my knee myself. If you come into my room, we both know what'll happen."

"And it's too soon," he said in an agony of frustration.

"I hate it when you look like that!"

With his fingertips he smoothed the distress from her features. "Hey, I'm a big boy, I've managed for three years, remember?"

"I don't even want to wait for three days," she announced with a violence that entranced him.

"Three hours?"

"Not three minutes!"

He laughed. "Back to your room, Rowan. Morning comes early."

She took three or four steps, limping awkwardly. Giving him a sly grin she said, "This is all your fault. If I hadn't been so preoccupied with keeping you off that plane to Toronto, I wouldn't have tripped over the curb." Then, as if her own words were replaying in her head, she paled and all the laughter vanished from her face.

Brant took her by the arm. "Rowan, there's something you're not telling me."

She made a tiny gesture to ward him off. "I can't," she said in an almost inaudible whisper. "Not yet. I just can't."

"You can trust me! I'm not getting on a plane to Toronto until the end of this tour, and when I do I hope to God you're sitting beside me."

"Please...let's go back to my room."

"One reason we divorced is that we're both as stubborn

as any of the donkeys we've seen on these islands," he said. "We've got to trust each other, Rowan. Not doing so is what's kept us apart."

"Are you going to tell me what your father was like?" she flashed.

He wasn't, no. "Stalemate," he said tautly.

"For now." Rowan ran her fingertips over the gray in his hair, her lip caught between her teeth. "We can't expect to fix seven years in half an hour. I guess."

"Trouble is, I was never known for patience." Brant swung her up into his arms, his one desire to remove that haunted look from her face. "You don't weigh as much as you used to. Or else I'm in better shape."

A tiny smile pulled at her mouth. She ran her finger down his chest and said, "Oh, you're in fine shape."

"All talk and no action," he grumbled, grinning at her.

"Most of the time I talk too much."

"While I don't talk enough."

"Tonight was a marked improvement on that score."

"How about we call time-out? I, for one, need to do some heavy-duty thinking…we'd be strapped for money if I quit my job."

She ticked off her fingers. "We could sell the condo—I sublet it when I moved to the country. We've got my salary. And there's your father's inheritance. We'd be fine."

"I suppose you're right…" For the first time Brant could see possibilities in the money his father had left him, money he'd vowed never to touch. He rather liked the idea of using it to set himself up in some kind of new career that had nothing to do with Douglas Curtis. The perfect revenge, he thought grimly, and heaved himself off the soft sand onto the path. Within minutes he was depositing Rowan at her door and she was turning the key in the lock. He said lamely, "You'll be all right?"

"I'll be fine. I'll put some ointment on my knee and go to bed." Almost shyly, as if he were a man she'd only just met, she cupped his jaw in her hands and kissed him softly on the lips. Before he could say anything, she slipped through the door and shut it behind her.

Brant scowled at the closed door, then walked to his own room, which was, of course, empty of anyone but himself. He sat down on the bed. He had a choice. Keep his job and stay divorced, or quit and be with Rowan.

But was it a choice? He had to have Rowan. He needed her. The last two years he had indeed been like a man possessed, doing his best—or his worst—to get himself killed. More than once he'd taken risks that had been plain foolishness, for which he'd have fired another man without a second thought. Even though he hadn't deserved to, he'd gotten away with them. But if he kept that up, sooner or later—and it'd probably be sooner—he'd step on a land mine or walk into an ambush and it'd be game over.

No choice at all. He wanted Rowan. In his arms. In his life. And to achieve that he'd give up a lot more than his job.

She'd never stopped loving him. Nor he her.

If he'd deceived himself so badly on that score, what else was he hiding from himself?

A five-year-old boy crying for his mother...

But Brant didn't want to go that way. He wasn't ready.

One thing at a time, he decided, and shifted gears. He'd miss certain aspects of his job, he knew that. The unpredictability. The excitement of marketplaces and dusty streets half a world away from home. The alertness to signals most other people wouldn't even see, the sense of living on the edge: he'd thrived on all that. Until the last two years.

Funny, he thought. Going to get Rowan this evening,

facing her on the beach like a man fighting for something incredibly precious, he'd had the same sense of living on the edge, of being in a country he'd never seen before. Rather startled by this similarity, he allowed his thoughts to carry him forward. He'd stifle in an office, and he was much too used to being his own boss to suffer anyone else ordering him around. An administrative job? Forget it.

He'd come up with something. Or—and again Brant smiled to himself—Rowan would.

He bent to unlace his sneakers, gratitude and a deep happiness welling through his whole body. Although he would have much preferred not to be alone right now, he was nevertheless content to wait. Because Rowan still loved him and he loved her.

His soul was in her keeping. He knew that beyond a doubt.

He was the most fortunate of men.

CHAPTER TEN

THE next morning at the ultramodern airport in Martinique, Brant went into the drugstore; he needed shaving cream. He also picked up a package of condoms, paying for both in American money and getting a fistful of francs as change. He had no idea if Rowan was still taking the pill, and he wasn't taking any chances.

She wanted children.

In the antiseptic cleanliness of the drugstore under its white fluorescent lights he was suddenly attacked by all the symptoms of danger: pounding heart and sweating palms and that knife-edge of alertness to all his senses. No job and a baby on the way. Was he crazy? Was the woman born who was worth that?

"Monsieur? Êtes-vous malade?"

"Non, non, merci," he said rapidly and walked back into the terminal. Rowan was standing in front of the machine that exchanged currencies, her face intent as she counted out the sheaf of bills in her hand. She was wearing bush pants and her dark green shirt, a slim, capable woman doing her job, a woman whom he loved body and soul.

He'd shortchanged her for the four years of their marriage. He'd given her money, possessions and a fancy condo. He given her all the gifts of his body. But he hadn't given her himself. He'd never given anyone that.

A five-year-old boy facing the big dark-browed stranger who was his father...

Was he totally out of his mind, or was he really embarking on the most difficult assignment of his whole life?

Brant shoved his purchases in his backpack and walked over to her. "Rowan..." he said.

A note in his voice brought her head around. "What's the matter?"

"Nothing," he stumbled. "I just needed to—hell, I don't know what I need."

"It'll be fine, Brant," she said vehemently.

"Do I look that bad?"

"I've seen you look better and I'm not asking you to do anything you can't do—I swear I'm not! Besides, I'll be with you every step of the way."

As if the man were still alive, Brant could hear his father's voice sneering at him. *Look at you—adventurer and world-famous reporter—leaning on a woman. Letting her put bars around you, cage you and coddle you, turn you into a momma's boy. You're done for, Brant. Finished.*

Rowan seized the front of his shirt. "Brant, don't look like that—I can't stand it!"

The voice had vanished. He was left with a distraught woman to whom he had nothing to say, and with Sheldon fast approaching them with a fixed smile on his face. He also saw how Peg and May were hanging back because they knew something was up, and how Natalie and Steve were giggling over some of the more risqué postcards in the newsstand.

Sheldon, who was oblivious to the possibility of any relationship other than his own, said, "We need help, Rowan, you know none of us can speak French."

"I'll look after it," Brant said curtly, and took off toward the newsstand, Sheldon in his wake. And if he was running away again, there were always times on assignment when retreat was the most prudent of strategies.

An hour later they boarded the short flight to Dominica. The plane was full; Rowan sat near the front and Brant

ended up at the very back. At the Dominica airport there
was a slight holdup with their van. About to wander outside
to examine the river on the other side of the road, Brant's
attention was caught by a small display of books in the
little kiosk by the entrance. He picked up a couple of espionage novels, both by a well-known author whose works
got rave reviews internationally. As he went to pay for
them, the woman at the register said pleasantly, "My husband, he loves those books. Takes him away from it all,
that's what he says." She laughed. "You can forget him
once he gets his hands on one, oh, yes."

"I'll probably be the same," Brant smiled. "Thanks."

The van had just pulled up; he went over to help load
the luggage. Rowan was doing the driving on this island.
They'd landed on the windward coast, where the ocean was
laced with white and where women were doing the wash
in the many small streams that ran into the sea. Banana
plantations and lush forest lined the narrow paved road as
they wound their way across the island to the west coast,
where their hotel was located. Rowan carried on an ani-
mated discussion with Peg, who was sitting beside her,
about warblers and parrots; Brant sat quietly, content to
watch the play of expression on her face and to let the
island's beauty soak into him.

The hotel was unpretentious and friendly, with its own
dark gray sand beach edged with tumbles of orange, cream
and magenta bougainvillea amidst swaying coconut palms.
Brant's room was at the very end, so he got the breeze
from two directions; his balcony overlooked the sea and he
felt instantly at home.

They all met at the beach for lunch. That afternoon they
drove north to the rain forest, where Rowan produced a
red-legged thrush out of the scrub on the way up the mountain, and then a charmingly plump gray and white warbler

at the forest edge. Parrots flew overhead, flycatchers darted up from the grapefruit trees, and again Brant was delighted to see the tiny Carib with its glittering purple throat.

They left just before dusk. The trail down the mountain boasted some of the biggest potholes Brant had ever seen. Rowan negotiated them with considerable skill; but he noticed she was limping when she came into the dining room for dinner. After they'd eaten, he got her to one side. "How are your knees?"

"Not bad. But it's weird, it's only nine-thirty and I feel totally wiped." Her brows knit in thought. "It was hard work, what we did last night by the rocks."

"High stakes."

"You said it. And we have to get up at five tomorrow, to see the other parrot."

"The Imperial parrot, otherwise known as the Sisserou," he supplied with a grin.

"I'll make a birder out of you yet."

"Now that, my darling, is pushing it."

She bit her lip. "When you smile at me like that, I turn into a puddle on the floor."

"When you say things like that," he riposted, "I want to carry you off to my room and make love to you until neither one of us has the strength to pick up a pair of binoculars. Let alone identify what's at the other end."

She widened her eyes. "You mean if we make love you won't be able to tell a hawk from a hummingbird?"

"Want to put it to the test?"

Her smile faded. "It still feels too soon, Brant—and I'm not being coy and I'm not playing hard to get."

It was the answer he'd expected and that, to some extent, he agreed with. At least, his head did. His groin was another matter. He said slowly, "Maybe I won't be convinced any of this is really happening until we go to bed together."

"I want to, oh, God, how I want to," she said helplessly. "But I'm so scared we'll do what we did so often—fall into bed as a way of escape."

"It doesn't help one bit to watch Steve and Natalie crawling all over each other."

"Or Sheldon and Karen necking on the beach," she added.

"Look at it this way—we're building character."

"We'd darn well better be building something."

He brushed her cheek with his lips. "Good night, my love."

She blurted, "Even though we don't really know where we're going from here, I want you to know how happy I am, Brant. Wonderfully happy and not lonely at all."

"Good," he said, patted her on the bottom, and got a drink from the bar before he went to his room. He stripped to his briefs and piled pillows against the bamboo headboard. Sipping on a rum as smooth as velvet, he opened one of the books he'd bought and started to read, doing his best to put Rowan out of his mind.

The next day was for Brant the most pleasurable so far. In the high Dominican rain forest they got incredible views of the rare Imperial parrot as it munched on fruit at the top of a tree by their picnic site; in the scope he could distinguish the individual feathers on the back of its neck, deep maroon feathers in startling contrast to its lime-green plumage. That afternoon he thoroughly enjoyed the boat trip to the cliffs at the northern tip of the island, stationing himself on the upper bridge along with the captain and Rowan. Back at the hotel, they ate callaloo soup and mountain chicken, and the sun set in pink and gold splendor over the sea.

He'd stayed up reading until midnight the night before; at eight-thirty he went to his room to pack for tomorrow's flip to Guadeloupe, and to try and finish his book. Rowan had driven Peg and May to visit birding friends who lived near the capital, Roseau; he wouldn't see her again until tomorrow.

Time was passing, he thought uneasily. Two more islands, and then he'd be heading back to Toronto. He didn't want to be alone in his room, he'd been alone in far too many hotel rooms the world over. He wanted Rowan with him. Now.

Besides, there was something she was keeping from him. A secret of some kind that was causing her distress. He couldn't imagine what it was; and knew it was adding to his sense of apprehension.

He needed to make love to her, to anchor their reconciliation in the body.

With an impatient sigh Brant headed for the shower. Afterward he went back into his bedroom, a towel wrapped around his waist. After uncapping a plastic bottle of guava juice, he picked up his book and his pen—because he'd been taking notes in the margin—and settled himself on the bed to read.

Rowan had delivered Peg and May to a bungalow high on the hillside overlooking the ocean, had met their friends and had enjoyed a piña colada made with local coconut. When the husband, a retired bank manager, offered to drive the two women back to the hotel later on, she accepted gratefully. She'd realized on the drive to the bungalow that she'd neglected to tell everyone what time breakfast was being served: a very simple and routine detail, the forgetting of which showed how preoccupied she was with Brant.

She got back to the hotel, gave the information to Steve and to Sheldon, and then walked down the path to the unit at the very end of the hotel. Her heart was thumping in her chest like a drum at a Christmas parade. Swiftly, before she could lose her nerve, she tapped on the door.

Brant opened it. When he saw her, his involuntary smile of pleasure went straight to her heart; hastily he snugged the towel he was wearing more tightly around his waist. "Rowan," he said, "I thought you were in Roseau."

Her eyes skidded from his bare chest to his long legs and then back to his face. "I forgot to tell you we're meeting for breakfast at six-thirty in the morning, the flight's at eight forty-five," she mumbled. "Sorry to disturb you."

His eyes gleamed with sudden purpose. "You didn't," he said, lifted her by the elbows, swung her over the threshold and kicked the door shut with one bare foot. Then he kissed her. Kissed her, she thought dazedly, as if there were no tomorrow.

Hadn't she, when she'd left him to the very last, hoped that something like this would happen?

She was tired of being cautious, of worrying about old patterns and of holding him at arm's length. There was nothing remotely at arm's length in his embrace, and she was going to make sure it stayed that way. Rowan threw her own arms around his waist, feeling the nub of the towel against her wrists, and kissed him back with a passion as instinctual as breathing.

Brant muttered her name under his breath, kissing her lips, her cheeks, her closed lids, roaming her face as though to memorize it. He smelled delicious, a tantalizing mixture of the familiar and the unknown, this man whom she'd lived with for four years, yet who'd become, in so many ways, a stranger to her. She dug her nails into his spine, loving the tightness of muscle and the knobbed bone, feeling his arms strengthen their hold as once again he sought her mouth.

Opening to him, Rowan let her tongue dance with his in

an intimacy that caused her heartbeat to spiral. She pressed into his body so that the heat of his skin penetrated her shirt, kindling a still greater heat. She toyed with his hair, traced the flat curves of his ears and the taut throat muscles, and all the while her certainty grew that this was where she belonged.

As though he'd read her mind, Brant raised his head. "Are you sure this is what you want to be doing?" he said roughly. "Because now's the time to stop if it isn't."

The pulse at the base of his throat was hammering against his skin; another drumbeat, she thought, rested her fingertip there. "I don't want to stop. Not if you don't want to."

"I don't have words to tell you what I want."

"Then show me," Rowan said with sudden urgency. "We've done enough talking for now."

He smiled into her eyes, dropping kisses light as raindrops on her face. "Not entirely. I love you, I need to say that."

"I love you, too." Giving him a radiant smile back, she said artlessly, "It's really quite amazing, isn't it?"

"Astonishing," he agreed solemnly. "I've got something else to say and it's very important, so you'd better pay attention."

She tweaked his chest hair. "You have my total attention."

"Good." He was laughing at her, she saw with a catch at her heart; he looked as young and carefree as he had on their wedding day and she wanted him as she'd never wanted any other man. "But you'd better hurry up," she added, swiveling her hips against his and widening her eyes mischievously as she felt the imperious hardness of his erection. "Or I'll be accusing you of being all talk and no action."

He lowered his hands to grasp her hips and gave a sudden thrust that made her gasp with a fierce and altogether unfeigned pleasure. "What did you say?"

"Skip it," she said faintly.

"You have altogether too many clothes on, that's all I was going to say. Particularly as the towel keeps slipping."

"You do have a way with words, my love." Rowan tugged at the towel, sliding one hand beneath to caress the jut of his pelvis and his taut buttock. "I'm all yours," she murmured. "Because do you know what I want?"

Again he laughed. "Me?" he said hopefully.

"Whatever gave you that idea?" Her cheeks flushed, she added, "I want you to undress me, Brant—the way you used to," and watched desire and wonderment chase themselves across his rugged features.

He reached for the top button of her shirt. One by one he undid them, his knuckles grazing her breasts, and all the while his eyes were trained on her face. She was still blushing, she knew. She also knew all her happiness must be written on her features for him to read. No barriers. No anger or bitterness. Only a deep joy that Brant and she were together again and that her world had righted itself.

He tugged her shirt out of her waistband and eased it from her shoulders, and only then did his gaze drop. Rowan stood very still as her shirt fell to the floor and he sought the clasp on her bra. It, too, slid to the floor. For a long moment he simply looked, his eyes stroking her flesh, lingering where her nipples had tightened like the seeds of ripe fruit. "I've never forgotten how beautiful you are," he whispered, and took her breasts in his hands, lowering his mouth to taste their ivory smoothness.

Her body quivered like an overstrung bow. Arching toward him, she began her own exploration, relearning the banded muscles of his belly, the hollowed collarbone and ridged rib cage, feeling in her bones as though she'd come home after a long and arduous absence. His towel joined her shirt on the floor. With a deliberation that was both sensual and wanton, she let her hands move lower down his body, following the dark arrow of hair to his navel, then wrapping her fingers around his shaft.

He groaned deep in his throat. Roughly he undid the zipper on her trousers and pushed them down her hips. His haste was contagious; Rowan kicked off her sandals, then yanked at the lacy underwear that she always wore on her trips as an antidote to the practicality of her outer garments. Hauling them down her thighs, she grimaced a little as she bent her knees.

"Easy, sweetheart," Brant said, "we've got all night."

"But I don't want to take all night. I want you now."

He pulled back the covers and drew her down on the bed. Hunched over her on one elbow, he ran one hand down her ribs, his face intent. She burst out, "I know you better than anyone in the world and yet you're a stranger to me."

"Maybe that's one reason I've craved to have you in my bed again—so you won't be a stranger anymore," Brant said.

Then she felt the slight roughness of his palm at waist, hip and thigh as he continued his exploration. For a few moments she closed her eyes, the better to savor pure sensation. Very gently he circled her knee; he clasped her ankle; he traced the arch of her foot where the blue veins lay close to the skin. Then, more slowly, Brant let his mouth do the journeying back from ankle to breast.

Shivering with delight, Rowan watched him, glorying in the intimacy with which he was traveling her body, knowing she wanted him to touch her everywhere there was to touch, so she could melt and yield, be filled and fulfilled. She whispered, "Oh, Brant, I do love you."

His lips had reached the peak of her breast. With exquisite sensitivity he played with it, until again she arched toward him in blatant arousal; only then, taking her head in his palms, did he kiss her lips with a deep and passionate hunger.

Rowan pressed herself to the length of his big frame, the same hunger encompassing her in its imperative and ancient demands; she ached and throbbed with that hunger. Suddenly, so suddenly that she cried out with an ardor as naked as her body, Brant parted her thighs and thrust between them. She surged to meet him, her whole being nothing but the frantic need to mate with this man who was her true and only lover.

He gasped, "Wait a minute, Rowan—are you still protected? If not, I can look after that."

As though he'd struck her, Rowan spiraled from a passion as scarlet as hibiscus, as searing as flame, into a very different place: an ice-cold place, a place of thick darkness. She pulled away from him in a single, graceless movement, her face stricken. "No, I'm not protected," she said.

Four words that brought with them a crushing load of guilt and sorrow. She shoved at his chest, as frantic to escape as only seconds ago she'd been frantic to join with him, tears crowding her eyes. As she fought them back, Brant said, aghast, "What did I say? Rowan, what's the matter?"

Her chest felt so tight that she could scarcely breathe. She tried to scramble off the bed and felt Brant anchor her there with a hand around her wrist. Like a manacle, she thought, tugging at it, a manacle of steel, and heard him say with genuine desperation, "You're not leaving—not until I know what's wrong. We can't run away from each other any longer, sweetheart, don't you see that? It's what we've done for years, me more than you, I know. But we've got to change, Rowan—or we're lost.''

He was right, of course. Certainly she'd been running from telling him a secret that had torn at her soul. She threw herself facedown on the bed as the first sob forced its way from her throat, and from a long way away felt his arms gather her to his chest. He said forcibly, "I love you. No matter what, I love you. And I'm not going to go away. Never again.''

But would he still love her, Rowan wondered, when he knew? Often over the years Brant had praised her for her honesty, told her how much he depended on her capacity to stick to the truth. But once, three years ago, she'd lied to him, quite deliberately, with consequences she couldn't possibly have foreseen and that had torn her apart.

How would Brant feel when she told him? Would he ever trust her again?

CHAPTER ELEVEN

ROWAN began to weep in earnest, her body shuddering with the force of her emotion as she plunged into that dark place of loneliness that she knew so well. She cried for a long time; and it took her a long time to come back to herself, to the reality of Brant's embrace, and of his voice murmuring soothing bits of nonsense into her ears. Gradually she became aware of two things. She'd needed to cry her heart out like that. Had needed to ever since she'd seen Brant at the airport in Grenada. And, secondly, this time she hadn't been lonely. She'd been held and comforted within the circle of Brant's arms and by the strength of his love.

She quavered, wiping her cheeks with the back of her hand, "I've got s-something to tell you."

He reached over his shoulder and passed her a box of tissues. "Blow," he said. She did as she was told, scrubbing at her wet cheeks and wondering if she looked as awful as she felt. He added flatly, "You don't have to be frightened. Not of me."

She hadn't realized she looked frightened. She said in a rush, her words rattling like stones in a stream, "Two or three months before you left for Colombia, I went to the doctor. He suggested I come off the pill for a while, for medical reasons. So I did. But I didn't tell you. I wanted a child so badly, and I thought if I got pregnant you'd be okay with it. You'd have to be."

A quality in his silence made her glance up. He looked stunned, she thought, and felt terror close her throat. "I lied to you," she said. "Not directly, in so many words—but it was a lie, nevertheless. I deliberately deceived you. And then you went away, even though I begged you not to…by the time you left, my period was three days late, I didn't dare tell you that, how could I? As a way of keeping you home? I wasn't going to play that game."

She blew her nose again, blinking her wet lashes. "After you'd gone, I went back to the doctor and discovered I was pregnant. You and I talked a couple of times on the phone before the abduction, remember? But I didn't know how to tell you, the connections were always so dreadful and I was so afraid of what you'd say…so I thought I'd wait until you came back."

"And then I got dumped behind bars for eight months," Brant said in an unreadable voice.

Because she was so frightened, Rowan spilled out the rest of the story without finesse. "They phoned me. From New York, to tell me you'd been captured and hidden away somewhere, they weren't sure where, but they'd try and have some news for me in a day or so. A day or so," she repeated, gazing at her trembling hands. "They might as well have said a lifetime."

Even through her fear, she was aware of the rigidity of Brant's muscles as he held her, of a quietness that was like the quiet before the howl of a hurricane. Hurriedly she went on, "I was upstairs because I'd been resting, I'd been having morning sickness and I was tired a lot of the time. As I put down the phone, the front doorbell rang, and I was instantly convinced it'd all been a hoax and it was you at the door, you'd come home, of course you had, I'd fallen asleep and dreamed that phone call from London. I ran for the stairs and I forgot about the carpet on the third step, it was rucked up, remember? I tripped over it and fell headlong down the stairs, and when I came to I was in hospital and I'd—I'd lost the baby.''

She was pleating the corner of the sheet with tiny, agitated movements, her lashes lowered. "I never told you. It was seven months before I saw you again, in the hospital room with Gabrielle. I suppose the miscarriage was one more reason I didn't go into that room to see you. Why bother telling you I'd lost a child you hadn't wanted in the first place, when you were—so I thought—in love with another woman?''

"My God...'' said Brant.

She risked looking up at him. His face was haggard, his gaze turned inward; she had no idea what he was thinking. "I cheated you,'' she said in a low voice. "I'm so sorry, Brant.''

He rasped, "I'm the one who was too busy to repair the carpet. You'd asked me to, and it would only have taken a few minutes. But I was too goddamned preoccupied with getting ready to go to South America to bother with something as mundane as a carpet.''

"It wasn't your fault!''

"You could have been killed.''

"Brant, *I* could have fixed the carpet—it wasn't exactly a difficult job. But I was too stubborn to, once I'd asked you to do it. Anyway,'' she finished with a flash of spirit, "this isn't about carpets. It's about how I lied to you and tricked you.''

Harsh lines had carved themselves into his cheeks; she was suddenly achingly aware of the dusting of gray hair over his ears. "It's about how you were alone when you fell down the stairs,'' he said in a bleak voice, "and alone when you came to in the hospital. That's what it's about, Rowan. I wasn't much of a husband, was I?''

She couldn't bear to see him blame himself. "You were

the only man I ever wanted to marry. Still are,'' she said
with the smallest of smiles.

"I never paid any attention when you said you wanted
a child. I was scared to death of having children, but I
didn't tell you that, oh, no, I laughed at you instead.''

"Brant,'' Rowan said vigorously, "we both made mistakes back then. Big ones. Are you saying you can forgive
me for getting pregnant without telling you, and then...''
her voice wavered "...losing the baby and not telling you
that, either?''

He stroked her bare shoulder, his face as naked to her as
his body. "Yes, I forgive you...although in all honesty I
don't think there's much to forgive.''

"I felt so guilty! You don't know how I've dreaded telling you, and yet I knew I couldn't have any secrets from
you, not if we're going to try again...maybe that's one
reason I was procrastinating going to bed with you.''

"You nearly told me by the rocks in Martinique.''

She nodded. "I was afraid you'd get on the first plane
back to Toronto.''

Brant pulled the sheet corner from her restless fingers
and trapped them in his own. "No secrets,'' he said
heavily. "In that case I'd better tell you that forgiving myself is a lot harder than forgiving you.'' He grimaced. "Can
you ever forgive *me*, Rowan?''

She lifted his hand and kissed it, her lips lingering on
his taut knuckles. "I already have.''

Briefly, he felt the prick of tears. Blinking them back, he
muttered, "You're very generous—more so than I deserve.''

She said emphatically, "I've learned something the last
little while, Brant...since we met in Grenada, I mean. It's
you I really want. Yes, I want children. But if I can't have
you, then nothing's worthwhile.''

He pulled her close, burying his face in her hair. "Let's go back to Toronto and get married again," he said in a muffled voice. "I'll quit my job and we'll do our best to start a baby, and somehow or other it'll all work out."

Her heart gave a lurch of pure panic. Wasn't Brant giving her everything she'd longed for—marriage, a different job and a child? So why didn't it feel right? Why was she still scared? No secrets, she thought, and said, "You should really want to be a father, Brant. It shouldn't just happen and then you'll make the best of it."

"Perhaps when the baby's real, when it exists, I'll understand what fatherhood's all about."

He didn't look convinced. Rowan said, "For now, I think we should use protection." She ran her fingers through her tousled curls, adding in frustration, "I'm the one who so desperately wants children, and I'm saying that? I wish to heaven I knew what was going on."

"I'm as yellow-bellied as a chicken," Brant said bluntly, "that's what's going on. The thought of having a kid—of being a father—scares me more than all the rebels in Colombia."

"Oh," said Rowan.

"So I think we should just jump off the deep end and trust there's water in the pool."

Rowan felt exhaustion wash over her. Brant was finally agreeing to start a child and she was telling him now wasn't the time. It was like the plot of a very bad movie, she thought wildly, one where there was no sense to anything that happened. She said with a stubborn lift of her chin, "I don't think we should start anything tonight."

He drew back. "You don't want to make love to me anymore?"

She glared at him, knowing she didn't look the least bit loverlike and not caring one whit. "Yes, I want to make love to you. No, I don't want to make love without protection. So there!''

"You know what I think we should do?" he said dryly. "Get some sleep...you look wiped, my darling, and five-thirty comes early."

"I sound like an echo, I know I do, but don't you want to make love to *me*?"

Brant grinned, guided her hand downward and said, "Sure I do. But I also want it to be perfect—we've waited a long time."

From a wisdom she hadn't known she possessed, Rowan said, "I don't think perfection is the aim here. I mean, look at us three years ago—a smart young couple with interesting jobs, two cars, an expensive condo—I bet we looked perfect from the outside. And guess what? We got divorced."

Brant's fingertip followed a tearstain down her face. "Real," he said. "Not perfect."

"Splotchy eyes, red nose and all."

His voice roughened. "Hair like fire, eyes dark as velvet and a body to die for."

"You know what?" Rowan said jaggedly, "I'd do anything in the world for you."

"Yeah? Then convince me you want me," he said, a gleam in his eye.

"No problem," said Rowan.

Her tiredness lifted as though it had never been, her smile combining mischief with provocation. Gracefully she rested her weight on him, feeling against her breasts and belly the abrasion of his body hair. She moved against him, slowly and with deliberate seduction, her hands roaming his thick hair, the width of his shoulders, the planes and angles of his torso. Passion flared in the blue of his irises; but he lay still, giving her the lead.

She slid lower, giving her fingers and her mouth full play, hearing him gasp in that mingling of pleasure and pain that she remembered so well. Then his control broke. Quickly he dealt with the foil envelope by the bed before lifting her to straddle him, guarding her sore knees; she sank down, filled with him, her face blurred with desire, her body melting with its heat.

What had been a game became an imperative. In quick fierce strokes Rowan rode him until suddenly Brant rolled over, carrying her with him, his big body covering her, his eyes glued to her face. "Now," he said. "Now, Rowan."

His deep thrusts had reached that place in her where only he had ever been. Her own rhythms surged to meet his until she was lost in the blue of his eyes, a blue like the blue at the base of a flame; consumed, she whispered his name over and again, like a mantra, and at her very core felt him pulse to his own release.

He pulled her to him, his heartbeat carrying her own with it in frantic duet. Then he said with the kind of honesty that's hard-earned and is consequently rare, "I'll never lose you again, Rowan, I swear...somehow we'll work it all out. We've got to. You're my life's blood, I can't live without you."

"I mustn't start crying again," she mumbled. "Not twice in one evening...oh, Brant, I do love you."

He kissed her, a kiss infused with loyalty and love. Rowan looped her arms around his neck, snuggled her face into his shoulder and gave a sigh of repletion. "I want to stay awake the whole night so I don't miss one single moment of us in bed together again, it's so lovely," she said, and within two minutes was fast asleep.

Brant didn't fall asleep right away. He settled himself more comfortably, enjoying the weight of Rowan's thigh over his own, listening to the small steady voice of her heart against his chest. He thought he might burst with happiness. Simultaneously, because he now knew how much he had to lose, he realized he was still deeply frightened.

Fatherhood.

Rowan was a child who'd been wanted from the time of conception, he was sure of that. He'd always liked her parents, two people of intelligence and strong will who'd accomplished that not so minor miracle of remaining in love through years of marriage and raising children. Rowan's sister Jane was a eye surgeon in a remote hospital in India; her brother was a biologist studying reindeer migrations in Siberia. Rowan's parents had loved all three children and had encouraged them to go free.

His mother had loved him. In his memory she was a pretty, frightened woman, nervous, edgy and overly protective; when he'd grown old enough to understand such matters, he'd wondered if she hadn't used up all her courage in leaving her husband when her only son was a baby.

His father had been very different. The several photos Brant had of Douglas Curtis showed a burly, dark-browed man scowling into the camera, surrounded by the corpses of whatever animals he'd just shot. Grizzly bears, mountain lions, Dall sheep, lions, tigers and elephants, the list was endless.

Douglas's house had been a taxidermist's heaven. Brant could remember all too well how terrified he'd been at the age of five of a polar bear that had been stuffed upright, its wickedly curved claws pawing the air, its gaping jaws set in a ferocious snarl. Not coincidentally, he'd done several articles in the last few years about poaching, big-game hunting, and the illegal trade in animal parts, a couple of them at some personal risk.

But he'd never exorcised his father.

He stroked the soft slope of Rowan's shoulder, awed, as always, by the silkiness of her skin. Her breath escaped in a little sigh, its warmth against his chest touching him to the heart. He'd protect her with the last of his strength from any danger, he knew that in his bones. So could he also confront the demons of his past for her sake?

He had no answer to that question.

It was late when Brant finally fell asleep; he woke to the beep of his alarm clock. Rowan reached over, slammed it off and yawned. Then she gaped at him. "Oh, my goodness," she said.

"A man in your bed," Brant said lazily.

As he gave her a hug, she slid her hips closer to his. "A man to whom bird-watching isn't a priority."

"Have we got time to make love?" he asked, kissing first one breast and then the other, his tongue laving her nipples; to his gratification she was already trembling to his touch. "I'm good, aren't I?" he said immodestly.

"Extraordinarily and magnificently good, and no, we don't have time, not unless you want the whole group to miss the plane and me to get fired for seducing a client."

"Wouldn't it be worth it?"

She gave a throaty chuckle. "It might be more than— Brant, stop that!"

"But I like it," he said, sliding his fingers deeper between her thighs and discovering she was only too ready to receive him. Swiftly he entered her, watching her eyes darken and lose their laughter in an ardor that inflamed him. Then she reached over and kissed him, stroking his lips with her tongue, her hips opening to gather him in, rocking to his rhythm.

Their surrender was fierce, quick and mutual. Panting, Brant said, "I swear tonight I'll show a little more subtlety."

"How am I going to face them at breakfast?" Rowan moaned, her hands to her flushed cheeks. "It'll be written all over me."

"They'll be too busy eating papaya to notice," Brant said, hoping he was right. He patted her on the hip. "You can have the shower first."

As she scrambled out of bed, she must have seen the torn foil envelope on the bedside table. She paled. "Brant, we didn't use any protection."

His swearword was unprintable, his dismay blatant. "It didn't occur to me—I was always used to you being on the pill."

"We've got to settle this whole business of having kids," she said violently. "We've got to!"

He swung his legs to the side of the bed and stood up. "What you mean is, I've got to."

"We've got to," she said stubbornly. "We're a couple now."

"It's a time in your cycle when you're not likely to get pregnant," he said in a level voice, "and we aren't going to settle it between now and the time we have to catch the next plane. Shower, Rowan."

She gave a sharp sigh of frustration. "Sometimes I hate my job!" she announced and stalked into the bathroom, shutting the door behind her. Brant took the torn envelope and buried it in the wastebasket.

When Brant arrived at breakfast, a discreet few minutes after Rowan, Rowan's gaze flew straight to his face. Her temper had vanished; he saw only love and anxiety in the dark pools of her eyes. He smiled at her, with neither the desire nor the ability to erase the love from that smile. Then he realized sheepishly that Steve was grinning at him, Sheldon looking puzzled, while Peg and May were exuding smugness. He stumbled, "Er—good morning. How did everyone sleep?"

Dumb question, Brant.

"Wonderfully well," said May. "How about you, Brant?"

He'd cut himself shaving because he'd been thinking about Rowan, and there were circles under his eyes. "Great," he said, and sat down. Rowan, he could see, was struggling with a reprehensible desire to laugh. He grabbed the coffee jug and filled his cup.

They all got to the airport on time, Brant sat next to Rowan on the plane, and at the Guadeloupe airport, a replica of the one at Martinique, the van was waiting. Their hotel was on the beach and his room was air-conditioned. As he dumped his haversack on the bed, the two espionage novels he'd bought in Dominica fell out of one of the pockets, along with the notebook in which he'd jotted his own plot.

Brant sat down on the bed, gazing at them, his brain racing. He was a writer by trade. Realistically, he also knew he was a very good writer: his boss wouldn't have tolerated him if he were anything other than first-rate. Furthermore, he needed a new job and he had enough money to tide him over a lag in earnings.

He'd write his own book. Heaven knows he had enough experiences to draw on for a dozen books. A whole series of books. He could even make a collection of some of his best essays and hawk that. The sky was the limit.

Excitement kindled inside him. If he could get a novel published, at least two of his problems would be solved: job plus income. Which only left fatherhood.

Leave the worst until the last, why don't you?

He glanced at his watch. They were meeting for an early lunch in half an hour. He'd stay in the hotel the rest of the day and tomorrow and get started. He'd have to do a lot more work around characters and plot; but he could do it, he knew he could.

Do it and enjoy it, he thought. Take a rest from constant tension and the seductive lure of danger.

Rowan was seduction enough for any man.

He locked his room and went to the main desk, where he found out he could rent a laptop computer from a company in Pointe-à-Pitre. In rapid-fire French he made all the arrangements to have it delivered to the hotel that afternoon. Then he bought a couple of pads of lined paper in the boutique, and went for lunch.

"Not coming with us?" Peg said, astounded. "But you'll miss the seabirds at Pointe des Châteaux."

"You'll come tomorrow, though," Meg said confidently, "for the bridled quail dove and the Guadeloupe woodpecker."

He said mildly, "I've got a writing project I want to start—I'll have to skip the dove."

"But it's a real coup to spot one," Peg protested. "They're notoriously difficult birds. And the woodpecker's an endemic."

"You can tell me all about it at supper tomorrow night."

"Dear me," said May, "are you sure you're feeling all right?"

"Never better," said Brant and grinned at Rowan. "A novel's hatching in my brain. Espionage, dictatorships and a good dollop of sex. The kind of novel that might just make a bit of money."

Her eyes widened. "What a good idea," she said.

"So good I can't imagine why I didn't think of it sooner."

"You've been distracted," Rowan said demurely. Then she began an entertaining story of how she'd dragged a whole group out of bed at four-thirty one morning expressly to see the dove, which hadn't deigned to appear until five hours later.

After lunch Steve grabbed Brant by the elbow and in a loud whisper said, "Congrats, man. Nothing like getting laid, is there?"

"You don't have to tell the whole world."

"I asked Nat to marry me last night and she said yes." Brant clapped him on the shoulder. "That's great!"

"You going to hitch up with Rowan again?"

"That's the plan."

Steve nodded sagely. "We're not getting any younger. Time to settle down."

Steve was probably ten years Brant's junior. "True," said Brant. "Give my congratulations to Natalie, Steve...I want to catch Rowan before she leaves, excuse me, would you?"

Hurriedly he took the pathway to Rowan's room. As she let him in, he saw she was gathering her stuff for the afternoon hike. He said, "As soon as I get back to Toronto, I'll call my boss and tell him I'm quitting. I may have to go over to London to clear up some loose ends—but I won't go anywhere else, Rowan, I promise."

She clasped her binoculars to her chest. She was, he saw, on the verge of crying. "I don't know how to thank you," she gulped.

"I'm past due for a change," he said awkwardly.

"To be able to sleep at night without worrying about you, to wake up in the night and know you're there...it'll make a world of difference."

This wasn't an opportune time for Brant to hear his father's voice taunting him. *She's done you in, hasn't she? Emasculated you, tamed you, domesticated you...how long before you regret this wonderful decision, Brant? You know*

*your boss well enough to know that when you quit, that's
it. No going back. Sure you're ready? Perhaps you should
reconsider...*

He fought the voice down and said, "I feel as though
I've put in a thirty-six-hour day the last twelve and I'm not
referring to sex. Whoever said love was easy?"

"Maybe that's why not very many people do what we're
doing."

"When this is all over, I'll take you on a honeymoon.
A proper one. Unaccompanied by birders."

"Moonlight and roses," she said dreamily.

"Gondolas in Venice?"

"They smell. I'd rather have satin sheets and candle-
light."

"Black satin sheets," Brant said promptly.

She giggled. "You're on." Then she wrinkled her brow.
"You know, I've been thinking...we're both trying to
change. But there aren't any guarantees, so we don't know
where we'll end up. That's pretty scary."

"We'll end up together, Rowan," Brant said strongly.

She flung her arms around him and hugged him with rib-
cracking strength. "I could bawl my head off again, which
is kind of crazy when I'm so happy."

"Off you go and find some purple-winged storks."

She laughed and looped her haversack on her back.
"Even Karen and Sheldon might pay attention if I did."

Brant kissed her thoroughly and with enjoyment, and
then went to his room. It seemed very empty without her.
He took out his new pad of paper and his scribbled notes
and determinedly began to work.

CHAPTER TWELVE

By the next afternoon Brant was both excited by the directions his imagination was taking him, and appalled by the amount of work it was leading him into. At two-thirty he decided to take a break and go for a quick swim; he didn't expect the others back for another couple of hours. He hoped Rowan had been successful in locating the elusive quail dove.

Rowan...she'd slept with him again last night, and they'd made love with a passionate intensity after dinner and with a languorous sensuality at two in the morning. As he strode to the beach, he found himself wishing her wedding ring wasn't in Toronto; he wanted it back on her finger, his seal on her publicly, their commitment restated.

Patience, Brant, he told himself, and plunged headlong into the sea. He swam for twenty minutes, feeling his head clear; with any luck he'd get another hour or two of work before the group got back to the hotel.

He didn't like waiting for Rowan. Even for a day. How had she ever managed when he was gone for weeks at a time to places like Peru and Afghanistan?

He'd been a selfish bastard.

But not anymore. He'd learned his lesson.

He waded to shore. A little boy of perhaps four or five was playing in the sand right by his towel. As Brant picked up the towel and wiped the salt from his face, the boy piped in French, "I'm building a castle."

The heaps of sand were lopsided and one of the tunnels

was in danger of caving in. Speaking French, too, Brant said, "It's a fine castle."

"Want to help?"

The boy's hair was brown and his eyes blue. Brant's hair had been that light a brown when he'd been younger. "Sure," he said, and knelt down on the sand. The boy passed him a green plastic bucket, which Brant packed with damp sand to make a tower. Before long they'd constructed a new tunnel and an impressive series of battlements topped with shells and scraps of seaweed. The boy's name was Philippe, he was five years old and he lived in Alsace.

Brant said finally, "The tide's coming in and I have to go, Philippe, I've got some work to do."

A wave tickled the little boy's feet. "The sea's going to wash away our castle," he said, his face puckering.

"You can build another one higher up."

A bigger wave rushed toward them, swamping the lower row of towers and gurgling into the tunnel. Philippe frenziedly tried to shore it up, but the backwash collapsed the last of the roof, leaving only a waterlogged groove in the sand. He began to cry, a heartbroken wail of protest. Brant said, giving the boy a comforting pat on the shoulder, "It's okay—we had fun making it and I'll help you start another one if you like."

His novel could wait. A little boy's feelings were far more important.

Then, from behind them, a man's voice yelled, "Stop that crying, Philippe! This minute."

Philippe flinched, trying to swallow a sob and scrubbing at his cheeks. But as grains of sand caught in his eye, his tears overflowed again. Brant took the dry corner of his towel and wiped around the boy's eyes, saying pacifically to the man who'd stationed himself beside them, "He got sand in his eye, he'll be fine in a minute." Then he stood up.

The man was unquestionably Philippe's father; he had the same blue eyes and wide cheekbones, although his face was choleric and his jowls flabby. Ignoring Brant as if he didn't exist, he shouted, "Be quiet—what are you, a sissy to cry for every little thing?"

"I got sand in my eye," Philippe snuffled.

"Sand in your eye, that's nothing—you'd think you nearly drowned. Quit your bawling or I'll give you something to cry for."

Almost the same words had been thrown at Brant time and again many years ago, hurtful, belittling words that, at first, used to make him cry all the harder. Only later had he learned never to cry, that tears were like the red flag to the bull and that feelings were to be buried so deeply they were never in sight. Standing up, his voice like a steel blade, Brant said, "You don't need to shout at the child—after all, he's only five."

The man glared at him. "This is none of your business—he's not your child. Stupid little crybaby, I thought I had a real son and I've got a mama's boy instead. But I'll make a man of him if it's the last thing I do."

Brant clamped his fists at his side and made a huge effort to speak rationally. "You're going about it the wrong way."

"When I want your opinion I'll ask for it."

"The way to teach your son courage isn't to shame him publicly," Brant said. "It's to show him your own courage."

Something his own father had never been able to do.

"Keep your nose out of the affairs of others," the man blustered, and grabbed Philippe by the hand. "You can go to your room, Philippe, until you learn to behave like a real boy."

Philippe was still sniffling. But as he grabbed for his pail he said with a flare of defiance, "Thank you, Monsieur Brant. It was a good castle."

"It was a wonderful castle," Brant said, "I enjoyed building it with you." Then he watched the two of them leave the beach, Philippe running to keep up with his father's longer strides.

If he'd followed his instincts, he'd have knocked the man to the ground regardless of the consequences. But somehow he'd had enough sense to realize that in the long run it would have been Philippe who would have suffered from such an action.

That whole scene was a replay. It could have been himself. Himself and his own father thirty-two years ago.

He felt flayed, every nerve ending exposed to the merciless sunlight. Memories that were insupportable crowded his brain, threatening to submerge him as the waves had so easily submerged Philippe's castle. Clutching his towel, blind to everything but a desperate need for privacy, because at some level he felt as vulnerable as a five-year-old, Brant started up the beach toward his room.

And then he saw her. Rowan, sitting on a beach chair watching him, her limbs as rigid as a doll's.

She must have heard every word.

There was no avoiding her. It was a good thing, he thought savagely, that she'd chosen a patch of shade that was away from the crowds near the pier. He kept going and when his knee butted against her chair and the shadows struck cool on his bare shoulders, said in a guttural snarl, "Spying on me, Rowan?"

She stood up with that coltish grace of hers, putting a hand on his arm. "Don't, Brant."

He shook her off, suddenly aware that he had a splitting headache. "I'm going to my room. Just don't follow me, not if you value living."

"I don't know what happened there, but—"

"No, you don't. So why don't you butt out?"

"I was *not* spying on you! We got back early and I went looking for you in your room. When you weren't there, I thought I'd try the beach."

"Why didn't you join me and Philippe?"

"I was enjoying watching the two of you—"

"Yeah…spying, like I said."

Rowan grated, "We're in this together, don't you understand that? That little boy was you, wasn't he? You and *your* father."

Brant's forehead was throbbing like a pneumatic hammer and he should never have eaten curried shrimp for lunch. "When I need your diagnosis, I'll ask for it. In the meantime, stay out of my life. Because it's *my* life, Rowan. Not yours."

The color drained from her face. "You're running away again."

With surgical precision he said, "Don't exaggerate. I'm only going to my room—not to Afghanistan."

"It doesn't matter, surely you can see that," she cried. "Please let me come with you, Brant. I won't say anything, I won't bother you—I only need for us to be together."

"No."

Behind Brant's eyes the hammer had reached bone, and he wasn't sure how much longer he'd be able to keep to his feet. He had to be alone; he craved solitude as a lover craves a mistress. But Rowan was speaking again, and through a haze of pain he heard her say, "You don't mean no. Tell me you don't!"

"I'm not cut out for spilling my guts all over the map. Some things are private, and best kept that way."

"Not if you want to be married to me," Rowan said, clipping off the words one by one.

"Your problem is you want to own me, body and soul."

"It's not about owning—it's about sharing!"

"Now you sound like that pup of a psychiatrist they foisted on Gabrielle," Brant sneered. Dimly he realized he was behaving unforgivably; and also knew he'd say anything to get Rowan off his back so he could be by himself. Anything at all.

For a long moment Rowan stood very still, staring at him, the shadows of the palm fronds slicing her throat and face. Then she said in a dead voice, "All this has been for nothing, then...our reconciliation, our plans to live together again. If you won't share your feelings or allow yourself to need me—we're done for."

And what was he supposed to say to that? "Just don't come looking for me. Not tonight."

"I won't," Rowan said, her chin high and her eyes like stones. "You don't have a worry in the world on that score."

"Good," Brant said, and somehow managed to steer a course around her chair and up the path to his room. He'd put the key around his neck. It was as much as he could manage to yank the string over his head and unlock the door. Slamming it shut behind him, he ran for the bathroom and lost what felt like every meal he'd eaten in Guadeloupe. Then, his knees feeling like rubber, he doused his head in cold water, took a painkiller and fell facedown on the bed.

Left alone on the beach, Rowan eventually got up from her chair and went for a swim. She felt as shaky as if she were recovering from the flu, as lethargic and dull-witted as she'd been after the miscarriage. Wincing away from that thought—from thinking at all—she swam back and forth parallel to the beach, her slow, rhythmic strokes gradually calming her. Only then did she go back to her room, shower, dress for dinner and make a couple of business calls. Finally she sat down on the bed.

She wouldn't be sleeping with Brant tonight. She was sure of that. But when she tried to whip up a rage that would sustain her through a dinner she didn't want and a night that would be crushingly lonely, she failed miserably. She didn't feel angry. She felt frightened and defeated and very much alone.

Brant had never, in the years of their marriage, talked about his father. It was a taboo subject, she'd learned that during their brief, tumultuous courtship when her innocent questions about his family had met with minimal information about his mother, and none at all about his father other than that the man was dead. At the time, she'd been so madly in love it hadn't seemed important. Now she was convinced that Douglas Curtis, killer of animals, had also killed something in his son's spirit.

His father was the one who'd driven Brant's feelings underground; had he also been the one who'd caused Brant to spend his adult life playing with danger?

Had his father shamed him as that horrible man on the beach had shamed the little boy called Philippe?

She couldn't answer these questions, questions that she knew were crucial. The only one who could was Brant. And he wasn't talking.

If he wouldn't talk to her, they were finished.

Around and around her thoughts carried her until, thankfully, she saw it was time for dinner. Brant didn't show up for the meal. She made some kind of an excuse for him and valiantly chatted with the group as if she didn't have a care in the world. Then May said, "We've been talking about our stay in Antigua tomorrow night. We saw all the birds on the list in our stopover the first day...the concensus of the group seems to be that we could go home a day earlier."

"I was wondering about that," Rowan replied. "I made a couple of calls, and I should be able to reschedule all of you out of Antigua in the morning. Should I go ahead?"

As everyone nodded, Peg said hastily, "It's not because we haven't had a wonderful time."

"You've done a brilliant job," May seconded, and again everyone nodded.

"Thanks," Rowan smiled. "I'll get on the phone after supper and see what I can arrange."

But what would she do herself? And what about Brant?

Rowan spent well over an hour on the phone, at the end of which she'd got flights for everyone tomorrow except herself and Brant, the only two Canadians. Great, she thought, just great. She and Brant now had an overnight stay on Antigua all by themselves and they weren't even on speaking terms. Top that one for irony.

As the leader of the group, she had a duty to let him know what was happening. As an estranged wife, she didn't want to go near him. The wife won, hands down. She fell into bed at ten o'clock and slept like the dead until the alarm the next morning.

Brant didn't show up for breakfast. Rowan waited until everyone else was tucking into fruit and deliciously flaky pastries before excusing herself to go and find him. Anxiety pooled in her throat, she tapped on his door.

Silence from the other side, and yet she was sure he was there. Was he playing games with her, refusing even to speak to her? Emboldened by a rush of temper, she knocked louder.

Woken from a nightmare in which he was being chased by a polar bear through a rain forest, Brant surged to his feet. The bed was rumpled, the bottle of pills still sitting on the glass table beside it. The digital clock said six forty-five. No way, he thought, it can't be that late, and flung the door open.

It was Rowan. She looked cool, crisp and capable. She also looked angry. But when she saw him, her face changed. "Brant—you look terrible."

To keep himself upright, Brant had grabbed at the door frame. He'd taken one painkiller too many through the night and was now paying for it, his brain fuzzy and his balance out of whack. Fingering his unshaven jaw, knowing his hair must be as rumpled as the bed and that his eyes were probably bloodshot, he said, "What are you doing here?"

Even to his own ears, he sounded far from friendly. He watched concern vanish from her face, to be replaced by a frosty reserve. "Breakfast," she said in a staccato voice. "There's been a change of plans. Because the rest of the group saw the birds in Antigua the first day, they're all going home this morning. But I couldn't get any seats to Toronto."

He rubbed at his forehead, wondering if he'd ever felt at such a disadvantage in his life. "Play that by me again," he said. "One fact at a time."

"Have you got a hangover?" she demanded.

"Painkillers. I had headache last night." Although headache was too mild a word by far.

"I see," she said noncommittally, and relayed the information again.

"So what are you going to do?" he asked.

She tossed her red curls. "I'll probably fly to Puerto Rico

with the rest of them and do some birding. You can do what you like.''

He was going to lose her, Brant thought in cold terror. Right now, standing here in his briefs looking like death warmed over, he was losing the one person who could give his life meaning. He said harshly, "Stay in Antigua. With me.''

"Why? So you can tell me one more time to stay out of your life? No thanks! Some of us know when to quit.''

His words came out without conscious thought. "I only got drunk out of my mind once in my life—the day I got home from the hospital in Toronto. The condo was empty, all your things were gone, and in the pile of mail was a letter from your lawyer saying you were filing for divorce.''

He moved his shoulders restlessly, wondering where he was going with this, knowing he had to keep talking. Although stray memories of what had happened last night were plucking at his brain cells, they refused to clarify themselves into any kind of coherence. God knows what he'd said to her. By the look on her face, plenty and none of it good. He labored on with painful exactitude. "The way I felt the next morning in the condo and the way I feel right now are about on a par...don't ask me what I said last night because I can't remember, but—''

"How convenient—now you've got amnesia.''

"I told you, I had a headache!''

Her gaze roamed past him to explore the untidy bedroom. "How many of those pills did you take?''

"I don't know—four or five.''

Her voice rose, her eyes blazing into his, "Maybe you don't remember what you said. But I sure do—and it's making Puerto Rico look pretty darn good.''

In a flash of insight that came from nowhere Brant said,

"Whenever my dad would yell at me, I'd try and hide. Run away like an animal to lick my wounds."

There was a small, charged silence. "Are you saying that's what you were doing yesterday?" Rowan asked.

Brant's knuckles whitened as he gripped the frame. "Yeah...I was running away. Trouble is, in those days there was nowhere to run. And no one else to keep me safe. Only my father." He looked right at her. "But now there's you."

In true anguish Rowan cried, "You've got to learn to stop running! It's too painful, Brant, when we're together as we've been the last couple of days and then suddenly you go away. Close me out. I can't bear it!"

He said roughly, knowing it was a moment of commitment that meant more than any wedding band, "I'll try my best never to do that again, Rowan. I promise."

She was staring at him, and this time the silence seemed to last forever, playing on all his nerves. If he'd lost her, he thought sickly, he had only himself to blame.

She whispered, "I've got to go back. The others will be wondering where I am."

"I've got a journalist friend from Antigua who owns a villa that he said I could use anytime. Let me see if it's available tonight, and go there with me. If it's not, we'll find a hotel."

"It was you and your father on the beach yesterday," she said, not very sensibly.

"Of course."

She was twisting her hands in front of her. "I'm like one of those boxers who never knows when to lie down. All right, I'll go."

"Thanks," he said hoarsely.

Rowan nodded, her face full of uncertainty. "You'd better get ready, the van's coming in three-quarters of an hour to pick us up...at least I only have to get through one more morning without all of them realizing about us.''

"Steve, Natalie, Peg and May already know. Karen and Sheldon don't care.''

"What?"

Rather pleased that she looked more like herself, Brant said, ''I told them.''

"You've got a nerve!''

"I must have, to be contemplating living with you again,'' he said with a smile that felt almost normal. "Rowan, if I've only got forty-five minutes, I'd better get moving. I'll meet you in the lobby.''

"Bring your room key,'' she said faintly, and turned away. Brant watched her walk down the pathway, her hands thrust in her pockets. Then he went into his room, closed the door and picked up the phone.

CHAPTER THIRTEEN

THE flight from Guadeloupe was uneventful. In Antigua there were a couple of hitches in the new bookings Rowan had made; sorting them out required persistence and patience on her part. As for Brant, he was doing his best to contain a raging level of impatience. Much as he liked May, Peg, Natalie and Steve, he couldn't wait to see the last of them.

Eventually, however, the six other birders were called to go through security for the American Airlines flight to Puerto Rico, which would connect to their various destinations in the States. Natalie hugged Brant. "We'll send you an invitation to the wedding and we expect Rowan to come with you." Then Steve shook his hand, giving him a man-to-man bang on the shoulder.

Peg and May hugged him more sedately. "If you sight a little egret, don't tell me," Peg said.

"They're not going to be birding," May said and gave him an innocent smile.

"You could time your next wedding for the Point Pelee migration," Peg suggested. "Then we'd come, wouldn't we, May?"

"We'd come anyway, Peg."

The migration, for which Ontario was famed, was in mid-May if Brant remembered rightly. "Plan on it," he said, and wondered if he was tempting the gods.

Karen and Sheldon smiled at him and politely shook Rowan's hand. Finally, to his great relief, they all headed for the security area. Steve was the last. He gave Brant a thumbs-up signal, draped his arm around Natalie's hips and disappeared behind the frosted glass.

Brant turned to face Rowan. As he stood on the sunlit pavement, surrounded by travelers and airport employees, he realized that, paradoxically, he'd achieved his aim. He was alone with her. Finally. He said abruptly, "The villa's available—Keith's away. The housekeeper said she could have it all set up within the hour, food in, the works. Then she'll vamoose." He hesitated. "You look tired out and I'm still woozy from those bloody pills. But that doesn't matter, not really. This is about us, about our marriage— even if we aren't married right now. It isn't about a perfect romance in a perfect setting, like an ad in a glossy magazine."

"Us," Rowan said uncertainly.

"About good times and bad—those vows I made so lightly seven years ago without having any inkling what they meant."

"I suppose you're right."

The smart thing for him to do would be to take her straight to the villa; it was a setting he remembered as idyllic, by far the best place to end the long silence about his childhood and to convince Rowan to marry him for the second time. His heart thudding in his chest, his throat dry, Brant grabbed her by the elbow. "I've got to tell you about my father," he said jaggedly, "it won't keep any longer."

"Here?" she said, glancing around her. *"Now?"*

"I've waited too long—seven years too long. I can't wait anymore, Rowan."

She looked, Brant saw distantly, extremely frightened, and somehow that strengthened his resolve. When he'd rehearsed this in his mind, he'd planned to give her a dry-as-dust psychological portrait of Douglas Curtis as a father figure, keeping himself safely in the background. But as he pulled Rowan back in the shade of a pillar, other words fell from his lips as though a floodgate had opened, an irresistible rush of words he couldn't have dammed up to save his soul. "My father arrived five days after my mother died," he said hoarsely. "I was crying when he walked in the room. Bad beginning. He had three rules. Don't show your feelings, never show you're afraid, and always push yourself to the limit." Brant leaned his spine against the rough pillar. "It didn't matter that I was only five and had just lost my mother, whom I loved. He had no use for tears, especially in his own son whom he was convinced his ex-wife had ruined. So he set out to educate me."

A plane took off behind them in a roar of exhaust. Beneath the noise Brant's voice sounded as rough-edged as an engine in need of a tune-up. "He lived in a barn of a house, full of stuffed game trophies, horns, antlers, tusks, you name it. Along with an arsenal of guns. He sent me to a private day school, where I had to learn to defend myself against the bullies. Defend and go on the attack. If I cried, I got shut up in the attic, which was gloomy and full of shadows and spiderwebs, and held all the animals that weren't in good enough condition to be downstairs—there was a boa constrictor that used to give me nightmares. If I defied him, I was locked in a dark cupboard—oh, hell, Rowan, I hate talking about it! It all sounds so trivial."

"Keep going," she said.

Her dark brown eyes were fastened on his face. Puzzled, he asked, "Are you angry with me?"

"Not with you. With him. And nothing you've told me so far is the least bit trivial."

"Oh…well, I soon learned not to cry. I also learned to hide my feelings, to bury my real self so deep he couldn't reach me…I never showed him anything that could be construed as weakness. He used to slap me around quite a bit—called it toughening me up, making a man of me. He couldn't keep that up indefinitely, though, because I had a growth spurt at thirteen and started getting a lot stronger...I moved out as soon as I turned sixteen and legally could be on my own."

Restlessly Brant rubbed at the back of his neck. "He taught me some good stuff, I suppose. I learned to be a dare-devil skier, a rock climber, a surfer. Whenever I mastered one thing, he pushed me to the next, always upping the ante...I guess somewhere in all that I got hooked on danger. On living on the edge as a way of life—that was the one feeling he did allow. Hence my job." He gave the woman facing him a mirthless smile. "It has a certain logic, wouldn't you agree?"

"Oh, yes," said Rowan.

"But do you see why I'm so afraid of becoming a father? What if I turn out like him? I couldn't bear to subject another little boy to that!"

"Brant, you won't. I watched you on the beach with Philippe, the way the two of you played together. The way you stood up to his father." Her voice shook with the depth of her feelings. "I think you'd be a wonderful father because you'd be so aware of all the pitfalls." With a sudden grin she added, "Anyway, you think I'd put up with the kind of garbage your dad handed out? No way."

A little of the tension loosened in Brant's body. But he hadn't finished. Not yet. "I think I married you knowing you'd be my salvation," he said harshly. "That you'd give me intimacy, comfort, companionship, everything I'd missed out on. And then I blew it. I acted like a carbon copy of my father, tearing around the globe proving what a macho man I was."

Rowan stood taller, her curls bouncing with energy. "But you were always so tender and loving to me in bed. That side of you didn't atrophy. Your father didn't—couldn't—kill it, no matter what he did."

"But I could only be tender in bed. Sexually. Not the rest of the time."

"That's changing," she said forcibly. "Besides, if it was only sex, anyone would do. Gabrielle, for instance. But it has to be me, doesn't it?"

She was right, of course. He'd known from the first moment he'd seen Rowan that no other woman existed for him. He wiped his damp palms down the sides of his jeans, noticing absently that the pavement was eddying with new arrivals, brightly dressed tourists, laughing and talking; they could have been a million miles away. Then Rowan put her arms around his waist and rested her cheek on his chest. "Thank you for telling me," she whispered.

Automatically Brant held her to him, staring blankly over her shoulder into the brilliant sunlight where an Antiguan family was milling around a pile of luggage. He'd done it. He'd broken all the rules his father had drilled into him, and described things he'd expected to carry to the grave unsaid. But instead of jubilation or release, Brant felt naked and exposed, as though he'd been staked out under a sun that had burned the skin from his body.

He said without a trace of emotion, "I arranged for a rented car. I'll get it so we can go to the villa."

Rowan looked up. Tears were glimmering on her lashes. "Brant, I can't—"

"Stay with the luggage, will you?" he interrupted in a clipped voice and pulled free of her, striding across the pavement into the glare of light. He was running away again. But he couldn't face Rowan's tears, the intensity of her gaze. Enough, he thought. Enough. He'd made a fool of himself, yammering on about spiderwebs and boa constrictors. A total fool. He should never have opened his mouth.

The clerk at the rental agency looked after him right away. He filled out the forms at the counter and couldn't have said two minutes later what he'd written. Then he walked outside, crossing the road, not even glancing in Rowan's direction. Some children were throwing a ball back and forth in the grass that surrounded the parking lot, their parents perched on white-painted rocks in the shade. He'd rented a red sedan; but when he tried to fit the key he'd been given into the lock, it wouldn't fit, and when he checked the licence number on the tag against the number on the car, they didn't match.

His fingers tightened around the key in a flare of pure rage. What had Rowan said on the beach in Guadeloupe? *You've got to share your feelings.* Well, he'd shared them, all right. And it had left him feeling worse that he'd ever felt in Colombia. Ten times worse. A thousand times worse. Passionately he wished that he and Rowan were like that perfect couple in all the ads, heading for a lighthearted romantic tryst by a tropic sea. No undercurrents, no battles. No past.

But they weren't. They were two real people instead. Two real people who loved each other, he thought, minimally heartened, and headed back across the lot toward the road. The children were now playing tag. He'd like to have half their energy.

Rowan had moved the luggage out into the sun. Her shoulders were drooping, her hair an aureole like a miniature sunrise. She was a woman of many contradictions, he knew that, for she could be fiery and gentle, capable and vulnerable. Yet ever since he'd met her, she'd fought him wholeheartedly with all the passion in her nature, because she believed in him and loved him.

Fight or flight. By telling her about his father, he'd chosen the very opposite of flight.

He waved the key at her, indicating the general direction of the rental agency, and was about to step off the curb when he heard a vehicle rounding the corner in a squeal of tires. A battered yellow van careened toward him, traveling much too fast. And then, to his horror, he saw one of the children, a little boy in a bright blue shirt, dash from the grass onto the road.

In a split second that was out of time thoughts tumbled through Brant's brain. Rowan was watching him. Once again she'd see him opt for risk, for danger: the very trait in him that she abhorred. She'd forgiven him the episode with the bull. But would she forgive him one more time?

He was risking all that he valued and longed to possess. Endangering his future with Rowan, the woman he loved enough to have bared his soul to her.

He moved like greased lightning, and even then, from the corner of his eye, saw fear transfix Rowan to the pavement, her hands flying up in the air as though to ward off what she was about to witness. In silence and in utter desperation Brant threw words across the space that separated them: *Forgive me, I've got to do this...I couldn't live with myself if I didn't.*

Then he lunged for the bright blue shirt, seeing a streak of yellow so close that in sheer terror he thought he was too late. Tires screeched. The stink of burning rubber filled his nostrils. He flung the little boy onto the grass, felt a glancing blow to his hip and struck the tarmac, from long practice protecting his head as he rolled into the ditch.

Silence fell, an instant of eerie and total silence. For a moment, crazily, Brant wondered if he were dead, because all the breath seemed to have been driven from his chest. Then the child started to wail, the mother screamed her son's name, the van door creaked open and footsteps raced toward him.

Rowan fell on her knees beside him, her hands roaming his body with desperate haste, then cradling his head. *"Brant*—Brant, are you hurt?"

He fought for air so he could answer her, the spiked grass

rough against his cheek. More people had joined her and a police whistle was blowing with excruciating loudness right in his ear. As though the jolting his body had suffered had also jolted his brain, Brant felt his mind suddenly open to a moment of blazing insight. Intimacy, he thought. That's the real danger, the one thing I'm afraid of. I have been for years, I was just too stupid to see it. It's intimacy that I always run away from.

It seemed truly ironic that—literally—he couldn't find his voice to share this insight with the one woman who deserved to know about it. Pushing against the ground with his elbow, Brant sat up, his head spinning. Swiftly Rowan lowered his forehead to his knees, her hands clutching his shoulders, and he took the first painful heave of oxygen into his lungs.

"The boy?" he gasped.

"Screaming his head off and not a scratch on him."

A babble of voices was surrounding them. Through it Brant muttered, "Sorry..."

"What do you mean?"

He managed to look up. "I did it again. Went for risk."

Rowan, who in the last five minutes felt as though she'd lived through a lifetime, said unsteadily, "I thought you were going to be killed in front of my eyes. The policeman wants to know if you can stand up or should he send for an ambulance?"

Brant had a horror of melodrama. "No ambulance," he said, and with the policeman on one side and Rowan on the other, staggered to his feet.

Rowan kept an arm around his waist, her eyes roving over him. He was swaying as if he were drunk, his face pale under his tan, his shirt smeared with grass stains and dirt. Wishing her heart would return to its proper place in her breast, she said with assumed calm, "How's your hip?"

He took a couple of experimental steps. "Nothing broken or sprained. For Pete's sake let's get out of here."

But first he had to endure the tearful thanks of the boy's parents, the voluble apologies of the driver of the yellow van, and the official questions of the policeman. It seemed an age before Rowan was finally settling him in the passenger seat of a red sedan, their luggage loaded in the trunk. Brant told her how to get to the villa and leaned back in his seat. The roadway was spinning in his vision, so he closed his eyes. She said succinctly, "You don't look so hot."

"Feel as though a whole herd of bulls has run over me. Rowan, I—"

"We're not going to talk about one single thing until we're settled in the villa and you've soaked in a hot bath for at least an hour," she announced.

"You sound like May."

"Be quiet, Brant."

Brant may not have been an expert on women, but he knew when to shut up. He drifted off into an uneasy doze, waking when Rowan turned down the driveway to Keith's villa. With crisp efficiency she escorted him inside and, against his protests, carried in their luggage.

The villa was nestled in a small cove; it had a red-tiled roof and white stucco walls, and was shaded by two tall African tulip trees. Trumpet vines and the pale blue flowers of plumbago clustered around the balcony, which opened onto a white sand beach and the jade green sea so typical of Antigua. The interior was cool, spotlessly clean and pleasantly furnished. As Rowan disappeared into the bathroom, Brant turned on the ceiling fan.

His hip ached and he still felt unpleasantly dizzy; various sharp twinges marked the parts of his anatomy that had connected with the ditch. But these were minor ailments, he thought, compared to the way he felt inside. Scared didn't begin to describe it.

He found shaving gear and some clean clothes in his pack and heard the water turn off. Rowan called briskly, "It's ready, Brant. I'll be in the kitchen checking out the food situation."

She didn't sound scared. She sounded as efficient and impersonal as if he were one of her clients, a conclusion that didn't help one bit. Although the hot water felt wonderful, easing the tightness of his joints, Brant soaked for much less than the hour that she'd prescribed. Wearing only a pair of shorts, he went in search of her.

The kitchen was empty. She was sitting on the balcony, staring out to sea, a bright red hibiscus tucked over one ear. "Rowan," he said, "come here." And wondered if she would.

Without a word she got up and walked into his arms. As he pulled her to his body, she whispered, "Your heart sounds like you've just run a marathon."

"I'm running scared—that's why."

Her head jerked up. "Scared? Of me?"

"Of us. Whatever that two-letter word means." Abruptly he let go of her, stationing himself with his back to the wall, his hands in the pockets of his shorts. "I had to rescue that little boy—are you upset because I opted for danger again?"

"Oh, Brant—of course not! How could you live with yourself if you turned your back on children in danger, or little boys like Philippe whose fathers mistreat them? That's utterly different from going off to Peru for two months at a time." Rowan riffled her fingers through her disordered curls. "I was proud of you. Truly proud."

Some of the tightness in Brant's chest eased itself. "I was afraid I'd blown it. For the umpteenth time."

"No way! Besides, even though no one ever rescued

you, this morning you were able to save one particular little boy from a terrible accident…because of you, he's alive and well. You could do a lot worse in this world.''

His throat tight, Brant mumbled, ''I hadn't thought of that.'' Looking straight at her, he spoke the simple truth. ''You're my rescue, Rowan. Only and always you.''

Rowan was rarely speechless; but for once, Brant saw that she was bereft of words. Without finesse he added, ''I want to go to bed with you. Now.''

Her grin was as lopsided as the hibiscus in her hair. ''I thought you'd never ask.''

''You still want me?''

''Why on earth wouldn't I?''

''After all I told you about my father…after the way I've behaved for so many years.''

''Brant,'' Rowan said, taking him by the hands, ''of course I want you. Don't you see? You're becoming just the kind of hero I've always wanted.''

''Huh?''

''You're hauling your feelings out of the closet to the light of day. You're letting me see you're less than perfect. That you're vulnerable. Don't you think that takes courage? Plus I'm finally starting to understand what's driven you all those years.''

''I've got another confession to make,'' Brant said roughly. ''All along the real danger's been intimacy—I figured that out while I was lying half-stunned on the grass and you were holding my head in your lap. Don't ask why it took me so long—some of us are slow learners, I guess. But intimacy's the one thing I've always run from.''

Rowan's eyes were suddenly swimming in tears. ''Little wonder, given your father.''

''So I haven't given up a life of risk, after all.'' He traced the softness of her lips with his finger, smiling at her. ''Not if I'm going to live with you.''

She was laughing through her tears. "And you have to ask if I still want you? You come with me and I'll show you how much I want you." Taking him by the hand, she led the way into the bedroom, where she pulled back the sea-green coverlet. Then she stood still, looking flustered and suddenly at a loss. "I didn't bring any sexy nightgowns. Didn't think I'd need them."

"You don't," Brant said. "Cotton sheets on the bed, though."

"White ones at that."

"Boring."

"Let's see what we can do to liven them up," said Rowan with a charmingly shy smile.

"Good idea," Brant replied, and took a deep breath. "If it's okay with you, we'll skip the protection."

This time two tears dripped from Rowan's lashes to run down her cheeks. "Oh, yes," she said fervently, "that's all right with me. Brant, I do love you so much."

Brant reached out for her just as she fell forward into his arms. "I love you, too," he muttered. "Oh, God, how I love you. It'll take me until I'm a grouchy old guy of a hundred and nine to tell you how much I love you."

"I don't want to wait that long," Rowan said pertly. "So you could show me. Right now." As she began unbuttoning the top of her shirt, the hibiscus tumbled from her ear onto the white cotton sheets. Brant picked it up, and when she had bared her breasts, he let the tissue-thin scarlet petals brush her flesh, his eyes holding hers captive.

In a low voice Rowan said, "Make love to me, Brant."

"Now and forever, I'll make love to you," he said, and with all the skills of his body and imagination, and with all the love in his heart, set out to do just that.

EPILOGUE

FIVE weeks later, as the first wave of warblers arrived at Point Pelee, Brant and Rowan were remarried in Toronto.

Rowan wore a simple linen suit with her rowanberry earrings, and carried a rather motley bouquet of orange and yellow lilies that made Brant laugh, so typical was it of his tempestuous and beautiful Rowan. Steve, Natalie, Peg and May were among the small group of friends and relatives who'd gathered for the ceremony. To his great pleasure his former boss had flown in from New York; he'd brought with him an offer from a well-known publisher for a compilation of Brant's best essays. Adding to that pleasure, Gabrielle was in attendance, as well. When she and Rowan had met the night before, they'd liked each other immediately.

The sun was shining. Brant felt extraordinarily happy. This time as he repeated the simply worded vows he understood something of their complexities and their demands, as well as their incredible rewards; and this time he knew he'd keep them.

At the end of the ceremony he kissed Rowan with all his fealty to her naked in his face, and heard Peg give a gratified sigh from the nearest pew. Afterward, as they drank champagne, he said to the two sisters, "I'm enormously flattered that you're here and not out at Point Pelee glued to your binoculars."

"We have a hired car picking us up after the reception," Peg said primly.

"We wouldn't have missed your wedding for the world," May added.

"Not even for a Bachman's warbler," Peg said.

Rowan twined her fingers with her husband's. "That, dearest Brant, in case you didn't know it, is North America's rarest warbler. We should indeed be flattered."

"Great party," Natalie put in, rubbing her hip against Steve's. She was wearing a fuchsia pink dress; Steve was having trouble looking anywhere but at her cleavage.

"Yeah," Steve said. "Kind of a rehearsal for us, eh, Nat?"

"By the way," Rowan said, "I'm afraid I won't be leading the trip to Trinidad and Tobago at the end of December—the one you've all signed up for."

"You won't?" May said in disappointment.

"Why ever not?" asked Peg.

Rowan smiled up at Brant. "I suppose the wedding reception isn't exactly the time to make this announcement— but by then I'll be eight and a half months pregnant."

"We just found out last week," Brant added, putting his arm around her shoulders and feeling her body curve into his. "So we've bought a house in the country—we don't want our children growing up in the city."

There was a flurry of congratulations. Then Peg said, "Of course you shouldn't go to Trinidad. Not with the baby due."

"Absolutely not," May said.

"There's no danger of that happening," Brant said. "She'll be here with me."

"The three of us," Rowan chimed in. "Home together."

HARLEQUIN ◆ PRESENTS®

THE BARONS

One sister, three brothers— who will inherit, and will they all find lovers?

Jonas is approaching his eighty-fifth birthday, and he's decided it's time to choose the heir of his sprawling ranch, Espada. He has three ruggedly good-looking sons, Gage, Travis and Slade, and a beautiful stepdaughter, Caitlin.

Who will receive Baron's bequest? As the Baron brothers and their sister discover, there's more at stake than Espada. For love also has its part to play in deciding their futures....

Enjoy Gage's story:
Marriage on the Edge
Harlequin Presents #2027, May 1999

And in August, get to know Travis a whole lot better in
More than a Mistress
Harlequin Presents #2045

Available wherever Harlequin books are sold.

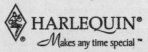

HARLEQUIN®

Makes any time special ™

If you enjoyed what you just read,
then we've got an offer you can't resist!

Take 2 bestselling love stories FREE!

Plus get a FREE surprise gift!

Clip this page and mail it to Harlequin Reader Service®

IN U.S.A.	IN CANADA
3010 Walden Ave.	P.O. Box 609
P.O. Box 1867	Fort Erie, Ontario
Buffalo, N.Y. 14240-1867	L2A 5X3

YES! Please send me 2 free Harlequin Presents® novels and my free surprise gift. Then send me 6 brand-new novels every month, which I will receive months before they're available in stores. In the U.S.A., bill me at the bargain price of $3.12 plus 25¢ delivery per book and applicable sales tax, if any*. In Canada, bill me at the bargain price of $3.49 plus 25¢ delivery per book and applicable taxes**. That's the complete price and a savings of over 10% off the cover prices—what a great deal! I understand that accepting the 2 free books and gift places me under no obligation ever to buy any books. I can always return a shipment and cancel at any time. Even if I never buy another book from Harlequin, the 2 free books and gift are mine to keep forever. So why not take us up on our invitation. You'll be glad you did!

106 HEN CNER
306 HEN CNES

Name	(PLEASE PRINT)	
Address	Apt.#	
City	State/Prov.	Zip/Postal Code

* Terms and prices subject to change without notice. Sales tax applicable in N.Y.
** Canadian residents will be charged applicable provincial taxes and GST.
  All orders subject to approval. Offer limited to one per household.
  ® are registered trademarks of Harlequin Enterprises Limited.

PRES99   ©1998 Harlequin Enterprises Limited

Coming Next Month

HARLEQUIN PRESENTS®

THE BEST HAS JUST GOTTEN BETTER!

#2043 TO BE A HUSBAND Carole Mortimer
Bachelor Brothers
It's the first time for Jonathan that any woman has resisted his charm. What does he have to do to win over the cool, elegant Gaye Royal? Propose marriage? But being a husband is the last thing Jonathan has in mind....

#2044 THE WEDDING-NIGHT AFFAIR Miranda Lee
Society Weddings
As a top wedding coordinator, Fiona was now organizing her ex-husband's marriage. But Philip wasn't about to let their passionate past rest. Then Fiona realized that Philip's bride-to-be didn't love him...but Fiona still did!

#2045 MORE THAN A MISTRESS Sandra Marton
The Barons
When Alexandra Thorpe won the eligible Travis Baron for the weekend, she didn't claim her prize. Travis is intrigued to discover why the cool blond beauty had staked hundreds of dollars on him and then just walked away....

#2046 HOT SURRENDER Charlotte Lamb
Zoe was enraged by Connel's barefaced cheek! But he had the monopoly on sex appeal, and her feelings had become so intense that Zoe couldn't handle him in her life. But Connel always got what he wanted: her hot surrender!

#2047 THE BRIDE'S SECRET Helen Brooks
Two years ago, Marianne had left her fiancé, Hudson de Sance, in order to protect him from a blackmailer. But what would happen now Hudson had found her again, and was still determined to marry her?

#2048 THE BABY VERDICT Cathy Williams
Jessica was flattered when Bruno Carr wanted her as his new secretary. She hadn't bargained on falling for him—or finding herself pregnant with his child. Bruno had only one solution: marriage!